KYLE XY
Nowhere to Hide

HarperCollins®, ®, and HarperEntertainment™ are trademarks of
HarperCollins Publishers.

Kyle XY: Nowhere to Hide
Kyle XY © 2007 Disney. All Rights Reserved.
Front cover artwork / photography (ABC Family / Andrew Eccles)
Back cover artwork / photography (ABC Family / Bob D'Amico)
Printed in the United States of America.
No part of this book may be used or reproduced in any manner
whatsoever without written permission except in the case of brief
quotations embodied in critical articles and reviews. For information
address HarperCollins Children's Books, a division of HarperCollins
Publishers, 1350 Avenue of the Americas, New York, NY 10019.
www.harpercollinschildrens.com
VIZ ALLATI
Library of Congress catalog card number: 2007928025
ISBN 978-0-06-143032-9
❖
Typography by Al Cetta
First Edition

KYLE XY
Nowhere to Hide

By S. G. Wilkens

Based on the series *KYLE XY* created
by Eric Bress & J. Mackye Gruber

⬛ HARPERENTERTAINMENT
An Imprint of HarperCollinsPublishers

1. The Laws of Nature

On Monday afternoon at Beachwood High School, Mr. Pierce, the balding, portly biology teacher, stood at the front of his classroom. He wrote the word *mimicry* on the board and stood back.

"There are a lot of species in this world that have extraordinary abilities to hide their true natures," he said, gazing around the room. Someone made a snoring noise. Someone else was making a new iPod playlist, concealing the device on his lap. But when Mr. Pierce pulled a giant photograph of a predatory snake from behind his desk, the whole class sat up with interest. The snake had a raised head, focused eyes, and its neck was fanned out like it was ready to strike. "*Cool*," a guy at the back whispered.

"Take this snake," Mr. Pierce said. "What do you think it could do to you?"

"Dude, that's a cobra," someone said. "It could paralyze you."

"Make your throat swell up," someone else volunteered.

"Send you into cardiac arrest," a final voice called.

"You're all wrong." The teacher smirked. "This snake's bite would hurt, but it wouldn't kill you. This is a *false cobra*—a perfectly harmless snake. It has, however, developed very special qualities: It can raise its head, spread its neck into a hood, and make a hissing noise just like a real cobra." He put down the first photo and held up another. It was of a snake that hardly looked any different from the first photo. "This is a real cobra. And, yes, *this* guy could kill you. Predators usually can't tell the cobras from the false cobras—so they think they're all poisonous. Pretty nice trait to have if you were an animal in the wild, huh?"

The class murmured in agreement. At the back of the room, one boy hung on to the teacher's words even more so than the rest. The boy had short, messy black hair; piercing blue eyes; and an intelligent expression. His name was Kyle, and by now everyone had heard of him. No one knew where Kyle had come from—not even Kyle himself—but word had it that Kyle was supersmart. He'd solved the math problem on Mr. Miller's board, after all—the one the MIT grad students couldn't even crack. By those standards, Kyle didn't have to take math for the rest of the school year.

Only, Kyle *wanted* to take math. Just like he wanted to take English and history and art and . . . well, everything. He loved learning. It was like his brain *needed* it, the way he needed food and water and sleep. And although Kyle was technically a sophomore, this was only his twenty-first day of school—that he remembered, anyway.

Kyle stared at the image of the real cobra. It reminded him of his earliest memory—which, since he suffered from amnesia, had occurred only two short months ago. He had opened his eyes in a cool, green, shady place—later, Kyle found out it was called Victor Falls and was right outside Seattle. A thick, pinkish goo had covered Kyle's entire body. He had no idea where he was, who he was, or even *what* he was. As he had stood up, a snake had approached, hissing dangerously. Somehow, Kyle had grabbed it and kept it from biting him. Kyle had no idea how he'd done it—there was a lot Kyle did that he couldn't really explain—but when Kyle let the snake go, it sulkily slithered away, as if Kyle had conquered it.

Kyle looked around the classroom. Mr. Pierce's scribbles were all over the board. There was a large periodic table poster along the back wall, and pictures of famous scientists—Einstein, the Curies, Watson and Crick—by the windows. At the back were the lab tables, and behind them were glass cases holding Bunsen burners, graduated cylinders, beakers, and centrifuges. Kyle was dressed like the other kids in the classroom—in a blue T-shirt; jeans; and blue, black, and white sneakers. His backpack, gray and yellow with a mountain peak logo patch on the front pocket, was identical to a few other boys' in this classroom. But while Kyle looked pretty much like everyone else, he didn't *feel* like everyone else. Not quite, anyway.

Kyle's eyes met Mr. Pierce's. The teacher gave him a tiny wink and a smile, and then put both of the snake photos behind his desk. "Okay, guys," Mr. Pierce said. "That's enough for today. Read chapter five tonight. It's about other mimicking creatures. I think you'll enjoy it."

The other students in Kyle's class began to pack away their books, when suddenly the PA speaker at the front of the classroom crackled. "Can I have your attention," a boy's voice boomed.

All the students looked toward the PA speaker. Kyle followed their gazes. His amnesia hadn't just made him lose his memory; he'd also seemingly lost all grasp of the rules of the world. He'd quickly learned to follow everyone else's lead, however—by doing what everyone else was doing, he could blend in. For instance, when kids looked at the PA speaker, Kyle looked, too.

3

He knew the speaker connected to a complex system of cables and wires that ended up in the principal's office, so whenever there was a PA announcement, it was always something very important.

"Attention, students. This is Justin Katz, your senior class president. I just want to remind everyone that Wednesday is the last day to buy tickets for the Monster Mash. So buy early and buy lots—and get ready for the scare of your life!"

As the PA clicked off, the class erupted with excitement. "Do you have your costume?" a brunette girl asked her redheaded friend a few desks over.

"I heard the haunted house is going to be awesome this year," a boy said to a group near the front. Kyle turned right and left, eager to ask what was happening—what was the Monster Mash?—but the bell rang and everyone jumped up before he could inquire.

Kyle shoved his books into his backpack and walked into the hall. People were everywhere. Kids pulled their books and coats out of their green metal lockers. A group of girls whispered near the black-and-white posters for photography club. Some guys jokingly shoved one another by the mosaic-tiled water fountains. Kyle felt dizzy. His most nerve-racking moments of every high school day were the chaotic times in the halls. There was so much to see and so much activity, his brain couldn't process it all at once.

Suddenly Kyle felt a hand on his arm and turned.

"Dude, we're in crisis mode," cried Kyle's foster brother, Josh Trager. Josh's animated face looked concerned. He zipped up his black hoodie. "Come with me."

Kyle hefted his backpack higher on his shoulder and followed. "Why are we in crisis mode?"

"The Monster Mash." Josh was walking really fast, pushing his way around people to get out the front double doors. Outside, the sun shone brightly, making the school's long windows, the metal flagpole, and the shiny chrome of the bikes on the bicycle rack sparkle. "We need costumes," Josh urged, widening his eyes.

"Costumes?" Kyle asked uncertainly. He continued to follow Josh down the school's front walk, past the large yellow school buses lined up curbside. "Do you *have* to wear a costume to go to this Monster Mash thing?"

Josh marched out the school gates and across the street, not even bothering to wait for the light to change. Kyle darted after him, narrowly missing a head-on collision with a red sports car. "Of course you have to wear a costume," Josh called over his shoulder in an exasperated voice.

"Why?" Kyle asked.

Once they reached the sidewalk, Josh stopped and took in Kyle's clueless expression. It was pretty much Kyle's *standard* expression. Josh was mostly cool with amnesiac, supergenius Kyle staying with his family until his real parents found him. The first few days after his mom brought Kyle home had been kind of freaky—Kyle didn't speak a lick of English; didn't realize that you *drink* tea, not eat the tea bag; and had no clue that nighttime was for sleeping—but the more Josh got to know Kyle, the cooler Kyle seemed. It was nice to have an extra guy around, too, since his older sister, Lori, had a little too much estrogen for Josh to handle by himself.

It was crazy, though, that Josh had to explain *everything* to Kyle, from how to use a fork and knife to what *Playpen* magazine was to which end of the Xbox

5

controller was right side up. In fact, Kyle had never even *seen* an Xbox before he set foot in the Trager house. Josh wondered if Kyle's real parents were the kind of people who homeschooled, forbade TV watching and video game playing, and didn't allow Kyle to eat any sugar—the kid was a serious fiend for Josh's Sour Patch Kids stash. Or perhaps Kyle's real parents were aliens—maybe sugar didn't exist on his home planet.

"Okay. I'll start from the beginning," Josh said slowly as they passed a strip mall with a diner and a magazine store. "The Monster Mash is this big party. A bunch of schools around here hold it together. There's a haunted house, a karaoke costume contest, an Elvis dance contest, this rad CGI graphics virtual reality booth, and all sorts of other stuff. And, yeah, you have to wear a costume to get in. But you know the *best* part of the Monster Mash?"

Kyle blinked. Josh knew he had absolutely no clue.

"The *girls*," Josh whispered, moving in close. "It won't just be girls from Beachwood but girls from Cedar and Fox, too. It's a major hookup scene." He shut his eyes, a hint of a smile on his face. *So many hot girls, so little time,* he thought. Maybe Ashleigh Redmond, the hot Catholic schoolgirl, would be there. Josh had met Ashleigh before school started, when the two of them had skinny-dipped in Jeff Preston's hot tub. Which had been awesome . . . until Mr. and Mrs. Preston found them. Josh wouldn't mind picking up where he and Ashleigh had left off. "This is going to be the best Halloween to date," he murmured.

"What's Halloween?" Kyle asked quietly.

Josh's eyes popped open. "Only the holiday that comes around every October? You dress up? When you were younger, maybe you went around to people's

6

houses saying trick or treat and they gave you candy? Is this ringing any bells?"

Kyle continued to stare at him blankly.

Josh let out a low whistle. "Just when I think you're getting kind of normal, Kyle, you go and pull something like this. You seriously haven't heard of Halloween?"

Kyle shrugged.

"Well, *this* is what Halloween's all about," Josh explained, gesturing to the store in front of them. A large awning said HALLOWEEN ADVENTURE in giant red letters that dripped down as if they were written in blood. A mummy, Dracula, a wolf man, a princess, and a hideous green alien glared at Kyle and Josh from the front window. All the mannequins stood in goofy poses, holding rats, spiders, and bats in their plastic hands.

"This is your source for all things Halloween," Josh explained, pointing to the entrance door. "My mom gave me fifty bucks to spend on my costume, but I guess if you see something you want, I'll split the cash with you."

"Thanks," Kyle said uncertainly.

Josh looked in the front window and pointed at a dummy wearing a silvery space suit and giant moon boots and holding a laser gun. "There. You could just get that costume and be done with it. I bet your peeps in their spaceship would find you if you were wearing that, huh? Maybe they'd beam you back up!"

"Ha," Kyle said, not really finding it funny.

Josh kept chuckling to himself. He walked into the store, and Kyle followed. Spiderwebs lined the entrance, and a giant tarantula lurked near the doorknob. Kyle narrowed his eyes at it, his heart speeding up. The spider looked dangerous.

"Dude," Josh said, noticing Kyle's expression, "that thing's fake." He reached up and squeezed the spider's middle. It squeaked. Kyle jumped, and Josh laughed.

They walked inside. Racks and racks of costumes surrounded them. A big banner floated above the store, saying SCARE CENTRAL, HALLOWEEN ADVENTURE! The place was swarming with shoppers, and some people were already dressed in costumes. A huge man dressed as a gorilla came up to Kyle and asked him if he needed any help finding anything. "I—I don't think so," Kyle stammered. He felt a little strange, talking to an ape mask. He wanted to see the person's face. He was about to ask, when he noticed Josh glaring at him from among the racks.

Kyle turned away instead, nearly tripping over a couple of pumpkins on the ground. He stooped down and looked at them carefully. Each pumpkin had triangular eyes, a triangular nose, and a jagged mouth. Someone had scooped out its insides and had put a small light at the bottom, making the face flicker. Kyle touched the edge of one of the pumpkin's eyes. It was surprisingly squishy. Kyle yanked his hand back.

"What are these?" he asked Josh, who was rifling through the costumes.

Josh stared at him. "Uh, pumpkins?"

"Yeah, but why are they here?"

"Gee, I don't know. Maybe because they're Halloween jack-o'-lanterns?" Josh's voice oozed sarcasm.

Kyle stood back up. He didn't even dare to ask what a jack-o'-lantern was and what it had to do with Halloween. It was simply one of those strange things about life that other people just . . . got. Sometimes Kyle wondered if Josh was right—maybe he *was* an alien. Kyle often felt like he had been plunked down on Earth from a faraway planet. Nothing was familiar to him. Nothing made sense. He couldn't remember a single thing before that sunny morning at Victor Falls with the snake. When he'd walked into Seattle, he hadn't even realized he wasn't wearing any clothes. He didn't even know what clothes *were*. He remembered that some cops had grabbed him and shouted at him, but Kyle hadn't understood what they'd said. They'd thrown a blanket over him, and in what seemed like minutes, Kyle was in a detention center. There, Kyle had felt scared, confused, and abandoned—and he didn't even know by whom. **KONTALKONTALKONTAL KONTALKONTALKONTALKONTALKONTALKONTALKONT ALKONTALKONTALKONTALKONTALKONTALKONTALKO NTALKONTALKONTALKONTALKONTALKONTALKONTAL KONTALKONTALKONTAL**

Luckily, Nicole Trager, a child therapist, had taken an interest in Kyle. While most of the people Kyle had met in those disorienting, overwhelming days in the detention center had been brusque, uninterested, and often frustrated that Kyle didn't understand the simplest things, Nicole had been friendly, helpful, and patient. She had spoken to Kyle in a slow, easy voice, trying her hardest to make him comfortable. After a while, Nicole offered to have Kyle live with her; her husband, Stephen; and Josh and his older sister, Lori, until his situation was settled. There, Kyle came to understand that he was a person, just like everyone else, and people are supposed to have pasts—child-hoods, experiences, lessons . . . memories. He learned he was supposed to have parents, too—people who had raised him until this point, who had looked out for him. But if parents were supposed to be caring and concerned, why weren't Kyle's parents looking for him? It had been two months since Kyle had come to live with the Tragers—shouldn't someone be searching for him by now? Or did they not want him? And why hadn't his memory returned, to give him a clue who they might be?

"How about this for a costume?" Josh said, snapping Kyle out of his thoughts. While Kyle had been daydreaming, Josh had slid into the dressing room and changed. Now he emerged in a white football jersey and purple spandex football pants. He wore a white and purple helmet on his head. All the pads in the shirt added about fifty pounds to Josh's skinny frame. To Josh, exercise meant playing a marathon session of Xbox and maybe casually shooting some hoops in the driveway—not running wind sprints.

"I look like a jerk, don't I?" Josh stuck out his lip and crossed his eyes. "Hey, where's my beer?" he said in a dumb voice. He looked at Kyle. "That's pretty much the only thing football players know how to say. They're all brainless jocks. At least the ones that go to our school."

"You definitely don't look like yourself," Kyle said slowly.

Suddenly a beguiling, flowery smell made them both turn around. A gorgeous girl stood behind them. She had a heart-shaped face, wavy blond hair, enormous blue eyes, and an hourglass figure. An expensive leather bag was slung over one shoulder, and she wore silvery high heels. "Nice uniform," she cooed to Josh, touching one of his padded shoulders. "Do you play for real?"

Josh quickly glanced at Kyle, then back at the girl. "Um, yeah," he decided. "For Beachwood High."

The corners of the girl's mouth spread into a smile. "Cool. What position?"

"Quarterback," Josh blurted out. It was the only position he knew.

"Niiice," the girl drawled. "What's your name?"

"Josh," Josh said in practically a whisper.

"I'm Samantha." She looked at Kyle and Josh. "Are you guys going to the Monster Mash?"

"Absolutely," Josh said quickly. "Wouldn't miss it."

"Good. I just got my costume." Samantha held up her orange-and-black plastic bag. Kyle could see something pink, frilly, and feathery sticking out the top.

"What are you going as?" he blurted out innocently. "A bird?"

Josh quickly stepped on his foot, causing Kyle to clamp his mouth shut. "Don't mind him. He's . . . new to the area. And he didn't sleep last night. So we'll see you there?"

"Definitely." Samantha whirled around and tossed her hair over her shoulder. "I'll save you some tequila, Josh."

"Great," Josh said. "Awesome. Looking forward to it."

Josh waited until she was out of the store and well down the block before he let out a pent-up breath. "Oh my God," he whispered, clutching his helmeted head. "Oh my God, oh my God."

"What?" Kyle asked.

"That was Samantha Jeffries," Josh said in a faraway voice. "The most beautiful girl in Seattle. She *models*."

He turned to Kyle, his eyes bright. "And she asked *me* if I was going to the Monster Mash." He pounded his padded chest. "Me! Every guy I know would do anything to go out with her. Guys throw their girlfriends

11

aside if she even *talks* to them."

Kyle gave Josh a once-over, from his shiny football helmet down to his bulky kneepads. "Would those guys pretend to be something they're not, too?"

Josh just shrugged, slipped back into the dressing room, and snapped the black velvet curtain shut. "Whatever. Anyway, I guess I'll have to find a different costume for the Mash now."

"Why?" Kyle asked.

"Duh, Kyle," Josh scoffed, "I can't go as a football player if she thinks I *am* a football player."

"But . . . I mean . . . you just said you hated football players," Kyle reminded him through the curtain. "You said they were brainless jocks."

"So?" Josh called. He sounded annoyed. "If it means scoring some time alone with Samantha Jeffries, I'll revise my opinion. And I'll pretend to be anything she wants."

"But do you really have to lie?" Kyle protested.

Josh peeked out of the curtain and widened his eyes. "Dude, stop the whole morality thing. It's getting kind of old. It was a white lie. Totally not a big deal." He tossed the football jersey and pants over the top of the curtain rod and slid the helmet underneath. It rolled clumsily and came to a stop at Kyle's feet. "Hang this back up for me, will you?" Josh's voice lilted out from the other side. "And then we'll check out Spook Land a couple blocks down. I hear they have better stuff anyway."

Kyle bent down and picked up Josh's helmet, feeling unsettled. He still didn't quite grasp the concept of lying. It seemed easy for Josh and Lori to lie—they often did about things they didn't want their parents to know. Even Kyle had lied once, to cover for Amanda

Bloom, the girl who lived next door to the Tragers, when she'd dented her car and was afraid to tell her mom. Even in that case, the lie wasn't easy; and in most other instances, Kyle didn't understand why people didn't just tell the truth. It seemed like lies always caught up with them in the end anyway.

Most of all, he couldn't imagine lying and pretending to be someone else to impress a girl. Kyle had a hard time understanding who *he* was—a costume would just complicate the matter. More than that, pretending just seemed . . . unfair. If you really liked someone, why would you do that to her? Kyle tried to imagine what it would feel like to do that to Amanda Bloom, who was often in his thoughts. Would Amanda like Kyle better, say, if she thought Kyle had a belly button? Kyle knew not having one was unusual—belly buttons seemed like one of the few things that universally linked all humans. Would Amanda think he was cooler if she thought he slept in a real bed instead of a bathtub—something he did for reasons even he couldn't explain? Kyle wanted Amanda to know who he really was, though. What was the point of being you otherwise?

As he strolled through the store, he watched as other kids tried on costumes. A guy emerged from the dressing room in a striped shirt and pants, with a broken chain around his ankle. "An escaped convict!" a girl near him squealed, batting her eyelashes flirtatiously. "I *love* bad boys." And a few rows down, a girl dressed in a colorful, skimpy dress; high heels; and a large hat with a bunch of fruit on top of it sashayed up to a clump of boys and started doing a Latin-style dance. "Can I have a banana, senorita?" one of the guys asked, and everyone erupted into giggles.

Without their costumes, they'd be just ordinary kids like everyone else, Kyle thought, pausing to watch the Latin dancer girl shimmy around the boys. Maybe people lived by the same eat-or-be-eaten rules of the snakes, lizards, and frogs he'd just learned about in biology class. People were just like the false cobras, hiding their true natures and pretending to be something else far more intimidating and powerful to survive. Maybe dressing up made people stronger and tougher. Better.

Kyle sighed and messily hung the football player costume back on the rack. It seemed like he'd learned fifty million new, confusing things about the world today. Then again, he had a feeling that he'd learn fifty million new things tomorrow, too.

2. Dress Up

Lori Trager and her best friend, Hillary Pierce, flipped through the racks at Party Haven in the mall. When a rap version of "Monster Mash" came on the store's stereo, Hillary started swaying from side to side. She pulled out a skimpy, sequined bodysuit and a pink sparkly wand and held it up to Lori. "This would look great on you, Lor," she declared.

Lori rolled her eyes. "It looks like Tinker Bell: The Slutty Years." She checked the tag. Amazingly, the tiny piece of fabric, wand, and crown cost $80.

Hillary examined it, narrowing her blue eyes. "I don't think it's so slutty."

"Your judgment is impaired," Lori teased, nudging her best friend with her hip. She glanced at the costume again. It had fluff around the armholes and neckline. "That looks like something a figure skater would wear. Everyone will laugh at me."

Hillary sighed, putting the outfit back on the rack. "Just don't go as a dead witch again, okay?"

Lori scoffed, pushing her long, wavy reddish hair behind her ears. "That costume wasn't *that* bad."

"Yes, it was," Hillary stated.

It was common knowledge that if a girl wanted to a) remain popular, b) get a date some time this century, and c) not end up on the various worst-dressed lists that floated around the school, she could be one of three basic things for Halloween—a sexy cat (or other sexy animal, like a bunny or a deer), a sexy princess, or a sexy devil. Two years ago, Lori had decided to buck the trend and wear something really, truly scary. She'd dressed up as a dead witch, wearing a ratty, black wig; a tall, pointy hat; a long, spidery dress; lacy black elbow-length gloves; and patent-leather witch shoes. She'd drawn gashes all over her face and big circles under her eyes with a thick eyeliner pencil and painted a trail of blood running out of her mouth. So the costume wasn't sexy. So she hadn't gotten any guys' phone numbers at that year's Monster Mash. So Hillary had been convinced that Lori had lost her mind and wouldn't associate with her all night, for fear Lori would "bring down her hotness factor." Dressing up as a dead witch had still been kind of fun. Since the Mash was the day before Halloween last year, Lori had even gone trick-or-treating in the costume the next day—and gotten tons of compliments on it from everyone who handed out candy.

Hillary sighed, changing the subject. "I wish we had dates to the Mash. Then we could just pick theme couple costumes and be done with it. Matching costumes are so much cuter, anyway."

"I hear you," Lori murmured, picking up a pair of pink satin devil horns and immediately putting them back down. The creators of the Monster Mash firmly stressed that the event was simply a costume party and *not* a dance, but everyone treated it like Halloween's prom anyway. Plenty of girls went with just a big group of friends, but it was much better to go with a date. After all, a girl needed a big, strong arm to grab hold of when she walked through the spooky haunted house.

"So who do you want to ask you?" Hillary said in a

singsongy voice. "If you could pick anyone from Beachwood."

Lori clamped her **781228** mouth shut. She had someone in mind . . . but she'd never say his name out loud. "I haven't thought about it, I guess. But whatever—no one's asked me yet. I'll probably just go by myself."

Hillary rolled her eyes. "Why wait for someone to ask you? You should do the asking!"

"No way." Lori crossed her arms over her chest. She passed a wolf man statue wearing an expensive leather jacket. The wolf's red eyes lit up and started blinking, making her jump. "I hate asking guys out. It's humiliating."

"That's so twentieth century," Hillary scoffed. "It's empowering to ask guys out. Sexy."

Lori didn't answer. If she asked the person she had in mind, she risked getting her pride hurt even more than it already was. How was *that* empowering?

Hillary browsed a basket full of wands, scepters, and tridents. Many of them were adorned with sequins and rock-and-roll studs and rivets. "So who's that cute houseguest of yours going with?" She shot Lori a naughty, flirtatious look and made a little tiger growl.

"Kyle?" Lori gave her a sharp look. "Don't go there. I mean it."

Hillary held up her perfectly manicured hands in surrender. "Chill. Is it a crime to ask?"

"Don't even *think* about Kyle. It's just . . . wrong." Lori sighed. She'd caught Hillary with her quasi-foster brother, Kyle, a few weeks ago at Jeff Preston's party. Hillary had been putting her typical I-want-you moves on Kyle—batting her eyelashes, running her fingers up and down Kyle's arms, telling Kyle he looked amazingly hot, the works—and Kyle had looked like a deer caught in her headlights. Normally Lori didn't care when Hillary flirted like crazy . . . but she felt a certain obligation to look out for Kyle. He was this freaky combination of special-ed kid and Mensa genius, and Lori wasn't sure he'd even *been* around girls before her mom brought him home to live with them. So she'd pulled Kyle away and, in the heat of the moment, called Hillary a slut. In retaliation, Hillary had dropped a devastating truth bomb about Lori and her sort-of boyfriend, sort-of friend with benefits, Declan McDonough. A truth bomb that Lori tried not to think about.

Lori sighed. And she *wasn't* going to start thinking about it now either. She plucked a feathery pirate hat off a mannequin, plopped it on her head, and admired herself in the mirror. She looked like her grandmother. "I'm sure Kyle's not taking a date," she said to Hillary over her shoulder. "It wouldn't even occur to him to ask someone."

"That's so adorable." Hillary swooned, clutching her hands to her chest and arching her back. "He's so sweet! Like a newborn!"

Lori shrugged. She took the pirate hat off, stuck it on a random shelf, and reached for a sequined flapper hat. "And if for some reason he did decide to ask someone, he'd ask Amanda Bloom."

Hillary's eyes widened. She took a step back, careening into a rack of Shakespearean maiden costumes, making the wooden hangers clatter together. "He likes Amanda? Did he tell you that?"

Lori shook her head, gazing at herself in the mirror. "Of course not. But I've seen the way he looks at her. And he totally lights up when she's around." She sighed dramatically. "Some girls don't even know how good they have it."

"But Amanda's got Charlie." The corners of Hillary's mouth spread into a grin. "Although I heard they might be on the outs."

Lori met Hillary's eyes in the mirror. "Where'd you hear that?"

"I don't remember." Hillary blinked, thinking.

"There's no way they'd break up," Lori declared. "They've been together forever."

Hillary rubbed her hands together. "This is very, very interesting. Kyle's little crush could create some major drama, huh?"

"Please." Lori rolled her eyes and ran her hand along a frilly, polka-dot Minnie Mouse dress. "There isn't going to be any drama. Kyle is so *good*. He'd never steal someone's girlfriend."

They continued walking around the store, running their hands over silk belly dancer outfits, satiny cowgirl dresses, and a hideous clown jumpsuit. Hillary returned to the Tinker Bell sequined bodysuit, tutu, and crown. "You know, this really would look amazing on you, Lor," she coaxed. "Just try it on."

Lori waved it away. "I need something a *little* more toned down than that."

Hillary sniffed. "You won't know until you try it on. You could look really hot in it."

Lori gritted her teeth and rifled quickly through a rack of capes. Hillary was constantly pushing Lori to loosen up a little, show some skin, flirt with more guys than just Declan. Maybe Hillary was right—maybe she should lighten up. She took the Tinker Bell costume from Hillary. "Okay. I'll try it. But I'm not making any promises."

Hillary grinned. "Awesome."

Lori pulled the dressing room door closed. Two ceramic black cats on the dressing room floor gazed impatiently at her, mid-meow. The tiny chair for Lori's purse was made out of fake bones. She slid off her top and pants, pulled on the bodysuit and skirt, positioned the crown on her head, and stared at her reflection. She had to admit—the costume looked amazing on her. There had to be trick mirrors in here—the sequined suit was cut high on her legs and held every curve . . . but in a very sexy way. Feathers hugged her cleavage, and the sequins somehow made her eyes sparkle. Lori thought she looked like a combo of a very fancy fairy, a fluffy Vegas showgirl . . . and a little bit of a slut.

"You're not a slut," she whispered at her reflection. "Seriously. You're not."

"How does it look?" Hillary's blue sling-back shoes appeared underneath the dressing room door. "Can I see?"

"I don't know," Lori murmured. "It's kind of bare." She could only imagine what her mom would say if Lori tried to leave the house in this. She'd definitely bust out her Therapist Voice, which was one part stern disciplinarian; one part empathetic girlfriend; one part wise, empowering older sister; and all parts irritating. *Girls who respect their bodies don't dress like this, Lori. You respect your body, don't you?*

"Let me see!" Hillary wrenched the door open and dragged Lori out into the middle of the store to the three-way mirror. She stepped back and clapped her hand over her mouth. "Oh my God, Lor. It's adorable!"

Lori looked around, trying to cover her butt and

practically bare chest at the same time. Luckily the store was empty, and the only salesgirl was behind the register, flipping through a magazine and chatting on her cell phone. Lori peeked at herself in the mirrors. "I'd never be allowed out of the house in this, Hill."

"Well, you *should* be. You look amazing."

Suddenly a movement at the front of the store caught Lori's eye. Lori glanced over . . . and her heart dropped to her knees. Declan was standing right outside in the concourse, next to the aromatherapy candle kiosk.

Lori looked around frantically. If she ran across the store to the dressing room, Declan might notice her. Instead, she turned and started booking it to the back, where all the high-end leather witch boots were. The feathers around Lori's legs floated up and down like they were all simultaneously taking a bow.

Hillary followed her. "Why are you running?"

Lori ducked behind a large mannequin of a knight in armor, a plumed helmet, and a flowing cape and caught her breath. To her horror, Declan was now walking *into* the store. He wandered to the side racks, pausing to pick up a giant, eye patch–wearing parrot. When Declan pressed a button on the parrot's stomach, the parrot squawked, "Ahoy!"

Hillary turned her head toward the parrot. When she saw Declan, her mouth dropped open and her eyebrows lifted an inch. "What's *he* doing here?"

"*Shhh,*" Lori said.

Hillary looked at her suspiciously. "Are you . . . hiding from him?"

"No," Lori said quickly, crouching down by the knight's boots, trying to make herself even smaller.

"I'm just . . ." she trailed off, realizing she had no logical answer.

"If you're not hiding, then I'm going to go say hi," Hillary said, taking a step forward. "Declan!" she called in a swooping voice.

"*Hillary!*" Lori pressed her nails into Hillary's arm. Declan glanced up from a bin of gawdy, blingy pirate jewelry and looked around the store, cocking his head. When he didn't see anyone, he shrugged and picked up a heavy gold medallion.

Lori faced Hillary. She bit her lip. "Okay, okay. So I'm hiding from him. I just . . . I don't want to see him right now."

Hillary knitted her brows. "Why? You're over him, aren't you?"

Lori paused. She'd had a crush on Declan McDonough for a long, long time. Miraculously, this past summer, Declan had liked her back, and they had a thing going. Well, *sort of* a thing—Declan sometimes snuck into Lori's bedroom at night, and Lori skipped her summer job to hang out in Declan's hot tub. They hadn't bothered to define anything, didn't exactly make regular plans, and never went out on dates like normal couples, but Lori really thought their sort-of-thing was going somewhere. They'd spent practically every day together, after all—how could it not?

Easy. Declan simply dropped her. By the time school started, they'd stopped talking. Lori felt crushed but tried to move on. Then, just as abruptly, Declan asked her to go to Jeff Preston's party with him. Lori was thrilled. She was determined to hold Declan's interest this time, which meant taking their relationship to the next level.

She had lost her virginity to Declan at Preston's

party. Lori unfortunately remembered every agonizing second—the spiny, dry grass on her bare back; the way the spot behind Preston's pool house smelled like chlorine and a stinky ginkgo tree; how a hip-hop song Lori hated had been playing in the background the whole time; and how, afterward, she and Declan had no idea what to say to each other. As they'd both put their clothes on and made their way back to the party, Lori felt tears rushing to her eyes. Wasn't her first time supposed to be special? Memorable? Sweet?

And then she had discovered Hillary draped over Kyle on the couch. When she pulled Hillary off Kyle, Hillary had admitted to Lori that the only reason Declan had asked her out again was because Hillary had told him that Lori was willing to go all the way with him. Declan had tried to deny it, but Lori knew it was true.

Now she watched Declan pick up an enormous bejeweled sword. He was wearing her favorite navy-blue polo shirt. His dark-blue jeans looked new. Lori wanted to ask him where he'd gotten them. And she wanted to ask him how basketball practice was going and if his dad was still acting like a jerk. Only, she was too proud to start a conversation—talking to him would probably make her look desperate. Instead, she willfully repeated a mantra in her head: *You're too good for him. He used you.*

"Of course I'm over him," Lori answered finally, her voice dry and thin. She looked back at Hillary. "I hate his guts."

"Good," Hillary said back. "So stop hiding."

Thankfully, Declan's cell phone rang. He answered it and drifted out of the store, heading down the mall concourse toward the exit. Lori waited until he was completely out of sight, and then bolted across the store into her dressing room. She yanked the door closed, tore off the skimpy Halloween costume as fast as she could, and slid back into her skinny jeans and fluttery purple top.

She glanced at her reflection in the mirror, breathing hard. She felt like Lori Trager again. On the other hand, Lori Trager was about the last person she wanted to be right now.

3. The View from the Top

That same afternoon, Kyle pulled himself up the last rung of the ladder to the Tragers' backyard tree house. He shimmied onto the tree house platform, found a comfortable cross-legged position, and gazed out across the green expanse of grass. Tall, shady trees lined the curbs. Kids rode by on their bicycles and skateboards. Kyle could hear the thump, thump of Josh's basketball hitting the pavement. A sparrow sat very still on the Tragers' roof. Kyle watched it for a moment. The bird stared at him, unblinking. Kyle smiled faintly, and the bird seemed to nod in approval.

Kyle had discovered this tree three weeks ago on his first official day of school, and he had been climbing up it every afternoon since. The tree was a great place to think—it was quiet, the air was cool and fresh, and Kyle could feel alone without truly being alone. For instance, right now, he could look into one of the Tragers' upstairs windows and see Lori in her bedroom, giggling on the phone with Hillary, just as she always did around this time. Josh was on the family's mini basketball court in the side yard practicing his layups, narrating his basketball game as he went—"Trager advances up the court, cuts across under the net, he shoots . . . he scores!" Josh would be at it for fifteen or so more minutes, and then would go inside and probably play computer games. Soon, Nicole would be home from her office and start to make dinner—which, since it was Monday, would be enchiladas. Stephen would be home from his job at the software company in an hour, unless traffic was especially bad.

Kyle smiled. He loved that he'd gotten to know the family's steady, stable routines. And it was so nice to have a family to call his own—especially the Tragers. They were all so balanced and understanding. Even though they all had their ups and downs—Lori seemed to be having boyfriend problems, Josh constantly got into trouble, and Nicole worried too much—they really cared about one another.

Which was why Kyle felt a little guilty about interrupting their lives. He knew his situation was weird. When Kyle first arrived, they'd had to watch him constantly, teaching him the simplest concepts and manners like he was a new puppy, freaking out whenever he got out of their sight. Stephen even brought Kyle to *work* with him once, and Nicole tried to counsel Kyle every day. Kyle had taken note of their faces as they fretted over whether he'd sleep at night (yep, once he discovered the bathtub and white noise on the radio), if his memory would ever come back (nope, not yet), and if his parents would ever come to claim him (nope on that, too). Even though the Tragers emphasized again and again that they wanted Kyle here, he hated to be a burden.

Kyle constantly thought about his memory and identity. Who was he? Why couldn't he remember anything? Kyle had only a few scattered, fearful feelings from before his awakening near Victoria Falls. One of them had to do with the man Kyle had seen briefly in the Tragers' foyer not long ago. Nicole had said later the man was Tom Foss, the new neighborhood cop, but when Foss's eyes locked with Kyle's, Kyle got the oddest feeling like he . . . *knew* him. But how? From the past? Kyle didn't want to mention it to the Tragers, though—it seemed like Nicole and Stephen didn't trust Foss. Nicole had even wondered aloud if Foss was a real cop or not—something about him seemed suspicious. Kyle agreed.

Kyle sighed and tried to push all those thoughts out of his head. He thought instead about the Monster Mash and Halloween. Halloween seemed like such a strange concept, yet everyone seemed to find it incredibly exciting. On their walk home from school, Josh had described to Kyle all the crazy Halloween costumes his mother had sewn for him when he was younger. Most of them sounded pretty complicated and gory. Kyle tried to imagine himself dressing up as someone or something else, but he couldn't. He sort of felt like he was in a costume 24-7—a *Kyle* costume. Somewhere out there was Kyle's true identity, the one he'd eventually remember. Only . . . when?

Kyle let out a frustrated groan. Even when he tried not to think about his lost memories, the questions always pushed their way back in. He knew he needed to be patient. Soon enough, his memory would come back, and with it his old identity and personality. And then he could go back to being himself. Or was he already himself? It was so hard to say.

A car door slammed. Kyle looked down and saw a familiar white convertible in the neighbor's driveway. His heart lifted when Amanda Bloom stepped out of the car, grabbed her blue backpack, and started for her house's side door.

"Amanda!" Kyle called out. Amanda looked around,

unsure where the voice was coming from. "Up here!" Kyle yelled.

Amanda walked to the foot of the tree and peered up. Her long blond hair danced down her back and her brown eyes sparkled. She was wearing a pink cable-knit sweater that showed off her flushed cheeks. "Kyle? What are you doing up there?"

"Just sitting," Kyle answered.

Amanda smiled. "I'm pretty sure no one's used that tree house in years."

"I know," Kyle said. Josh had told him that he'd abandoned the tree house after elementary school. "But it still seems pretty sturdy. And the ladder still works. Want to come up?"

Amanda paused. She looked over her shoulder into her house. "Why not?" she said, and started climbing.

When she reached the last rung, Kyle stretched out his hand to help her onto the platform. As soon as Amanda touched him, Kyle felt an electrifying force flow through his body. Amanda's big brown eyes met his, and she let out a small giggle. Kyle tried to laugh back, but the noise got stuck in his throat and sounded sort of froggish and tortured. When Amanda dropped his hand and scooted onto the platform to sit down, the electrical charge didn't go away. Kyle glanced at his hand, wondering if something miraculous had happened to it just from touching her—perhaps it was now multicolored or robotic or see-through. But, no, it was still his plain hand, same as it always was.

"This is great." Amanda squinted over the treetops. "I always wanted to come up here, but Josh never let me. No girls were allowed. He had a big sign and everything."

Kyle smirked. "Nowadays Josh would invite up all the girls this tree house could hold."

"Probably." Amanda giggled.

"So how are you?" Kyle asked.

"I'm okay," Amanda said. She leaned back on her elbows and sighed heavily. "That's such a lie. Actually, I'm really stressed out."

"Why?"

"I'm in charge of the decorations for the Monster Mash," Amanda explained. "And . . . I'm really behind. My whole committee bailed on me to go work on the haunted house." She rubbed her eyes. "I have no idea how I'm going to have everything ready for Saturday."

"Can I help?" Kyle blurted out.

Amanda looked over, surprised. "For real?"

"Sure."

"It wouldn't be hard. Just blowing up balloons, hanging streamers, and painting this mural—which is perfect, because your drawings are awesome."

Kyle blushed. Drawing came naturally to him—he just duplicated what he saw in his head. "I'd be happy to help."

The truth was, Kyle would do anything for extra time with Amanda. He had met her when he'd known nothing about the world, by following the sound of Amanda's piano music straight into her house. He had thought Amanda was some sort of magical goddess, able to create the most beautiful sounds with just her fingers. And when Amanda had turned around to look at Kyle for the first time, a light had turned on inside him. When Kyle was around Amanda, he felt like he could say absolutely anything and that Amanda would understand. He felt like . . . himself.

The only problem was, Amanda had a boyfriend. Charlie.

"You're a lifesaver," Amanda said, bringing Kyle back to the present. To Kyle's surprise, she flung her arms around his neck. She smelled like strawberry soap, and her body felt willowy and slight. When they pulled away, Kyle felt a light-headed rush of bravery. *Maybe I should tell her how I feel when I'm around her,* he thought. He had held back before—he knew it would complicate things, since Amanda was with Charlie. It might even disturb their friendship. But at least Amanda would know. It would be out there.

Kyle took a deep breath. "Amanda, I—"

"Amanda?" a voice called from below, interrupting him. Kyle looked into the yard. Amanda's mother, Mrs. Bloom, was standing on the side porch. As usual, she looked very polished. Not a blond hair was out of place, her pearls sat perfectly on her neck, and her tweed jacket and pants fit as if the designer had sewn them especially for her. "Where are you?" she called.

Amanda glanced at Kyle. "I should go," she whispered. "I'm sure she wants me to do five billion chores."

"Are you okay getting down?" Kyle asked.

"I'm fine." Amanda smiled at him. "So want to meet me at the Beachwood Rec Center tomorrow? It's not far from the school. Lori or Josh can tell you how to get there. I'll bring all the decorations."

"I'll be there," Kyle answered shakily.

Amanda threw him a winning grin, then scurried down the ladder. Kyle watched as she pranced across the yard to her mom. Mrs. Bloom took one baffled look at Amanda, then craned her neck to look at Kyle in the tree.

"What were you doing with him?" Mrs. Bloom hissed. She had taken a dislike to Kyle right away, after he'd walked into her house without being invited. She'd thought Kyle was a stalker.

"We were just talking," Amanda said in an irritated voice, pushing her hair over her shoulder and walking toward her side door.

"I don't know what you two would have to talk about," Mrs. Bloom tutted. Before following her daughter inside, she glanced up at the tree again and narrowed her eyes. Kyle gave her a shallow wave, but she didn't wave back.

Once they shut their door, Kyle put his head in his hands. He felt sweaty and dizzy. He was *this close* to telling Amanda how he felt. What if he had—and she laughed at him? Or worse—what if she had gotten angry? He breathed heavily for a few seconds, feeling like he'd just narrowly averted disaster.

The sun dipped into the trees. Kyle sighed and slid off the tree house platform and positioned his feet on the first ladder rung, ready to go back inside the house. He stared down at the patchy grass and dirt below him. The jump wasn't that far. He could make it. It beat climbing down all the rungs, anyway.

He let go of the trunk and fell through the air. He hit the ground lightly, with perfect balance.

"Whoa," came a voice from the driveway. Kyle looked up and saw Josh staring at him, an orange basketball balanced in his hand. Josh widened his eyes, and then ran into the garage. "Mom!" Kyle heard him yell. "You won't believe what freakazoid Kyle just did!"

Kyle was about to follow Josh, but then he heard a twig snap. He turned around and faced the back of the Tragers' property. Something moved in the bushes by the Tragers' garden shed. Was that . . . a person? Kyle saw a flash of blue windbreaker, the white of someone's eyes.

"Hello?" Kyle asked. He heard leaves rustling. No one answered.

He walked toward the woods, but by the time he got there, whoever it was had vanished. Kyle looked around, listening. All he heard were birds chirping, the wind brushing the tree branches together, and someone's motorcycle starting up far off in the distance. But he had an eerie, prickly feeling at the back of his neck, like whoever had been there was still close.

Then he noticed an unfamiliar object nestled in the long grass that bordered the shed. Kyle bent down. It was a plastic, rectangular key fob. Stephen had a similar-looking thing for his office e-mail account, and like Stephen's fob, this one had a little LED window in the center that displayed six random numbers. Kyle watched the screen. 228756. In fifteen seconds, the six digits changed: 917849. In another fifteen seconds they changed again: 407283. There was no pattern to them.

Kyle picked up the fob. It felt a bit warm and clammy, like it had been in someone's hand. Besides the numbers, there was nothing else on the fob. No fingerprints, keychain, or other distinguishing marks.

He stared into the woods. The prickly feeling at the back of his neck was gone. It seemed like whoever had been watching him had gone, too. Kyle considered yelling *Hey! You dropped something!* but he decided against it. For one thing, he wasn't sure he wanted to give the key fob back. And for the other, he wasn't sure he wanted to meet whoever was watching him. He slipped the fob in his pocket and headed back to the house.

A stocky, unshaven man in a blue windbreaker sprinted through the distant trees, darted through someone's backyard, and emerged on a quiet neighborhood street. He bent over, putting his hands on his knees and breathing hard. Then he looked around to see if anyone was following him. The coast was clear. He brought out his cell phone and punched in a number. After a pause, he cleared his throat.

"It's Foss," he said into the phone. "I was just there . . . watching him. But I was afraid he was going to see me. I had to leave."

"You'll go back though, right?" the voice on the other end said.

"Of course," Foss answered. "First thing tomorrow. As always." He snapped his phone shut and jogged away.

4. It's Better to Forget

Nicole Trager pulled a pan of enchiladas out of the oven and set it on top of the stove. "Lori?" she called to her daughter, who was sitting in one of the wicker chairs in the breakfast nook, staring at a magazine. "Can you grab the salsa from the fridge?"

Lori didn't answer. She was examining a two-page ad for body spray. The tall, brown-haired model looked a little like Declan. He even had Declan's sly, flirty smile. Or maybe he didn't. Or maybe *every* guy these days reminded her of Declan.

"Lori?" her mother said again. "Earth to Lori?"

Lori blinked, shut her magazine, and turned around. "Huh?"

Her mother took off her red-checkered oven mitts and put them on the kitchen island. She gave Lori a concerned look. "Are you all right? You seem really . . . distant."

"I'm fine," Lori said quickly, sitting up straighter.

"Are you sure?" her mother goaded.

Lori picked at some flaky nail polish on her thumb. She got along with her mom pretty well—she wasn't overstrict and bitter like Amanda Bloom's mom was, and she had a pretty decent sense of humor. Lori thought it was a little bizarre that her mom had a rescuing fixation—she wanted to save everything, from the motherless bunnies in the backyard to spiders she found in her shower, and now she was bringing home her *patients*—but she forgave her mom for even that, now that Kyle was speaking in complete sentences.

It didn't mean, however, that Lori told her mom everything. And she certainly wasn't going to divulge the Declan Disaster, as she was now calling it. Lori could just imagine her mom's face if she casually laid out all the details right now: *Actually, Mom, I'm not okay. Remember Declan? You met him once or twice? You asked me if he was a good guy? Well, he used me for sex a while ago, and we really haven't talked since. But because I'm a complete and utter loser, I actually still like him! Now, what did you need from the fridge? Salsa?*

Luckily Josh burst into the kitchen like a whirlwind, cutting the conversation short. "He's going for the sixty-yard line . . . and touchdown!" Josh held his arms up, jumped up and down, and made cheering noises.

Lori wrinkled her nose at him. "Since when are you interested in football?"

Josh shrugged. "I like football."

Lori rolled her eyes and jumped up, helping her mom get the silverware from the drawer. "For the record, then, when a player is close to a touchdown, he's on the *zero* yard line, not the sixty."

"I knew that," Josh said quickly. "I was just testing all of you."

Just then Mrs. Trager looked up. "Hi, Kyle," she said.

Kyle stood in the doorway, watching Lori and Josh set the table. "Hi," he said quietly.

He cupped his hand around the plastic key fob he'd found in the yard, wondering if he should show it to Nicole. It might be hers or Stephen's—although he was certain the fob that linked to Stephen's e-mail account was black and green, not red and blue. Kyle slid the fob back into his pocket. He had a sinking feeling the fob belonged to whomever had been lurking at the back of their property. He would wait to tell the Tragers, though—bringing it up right now would probably just ruin the family's pleasant dinner.

Nicole looked at Kyle sternly. "Josh told me you jumped down from the tree house earlier. Kyle, what were you thinking? You could've gotten seriously hurt!"

Kyle blinked. He hadn't realized it was such a strange thing to do. "I'm sorry."

Stephen Trager came into the kitchen, a rolled-up newspaper under his arm. "Just don't do it again, okay?" he said to Kyle, having heard their conversation. "When Josh used to hang out in his tree house, Nicole practically had an ambulance waiting at the curb in case he fell."

"Well, it's dangerous," Nicole said uneasily.

Stephen kissed Nicole hello, ruffled Josh's hair, squeezed Lori's shoulder, and patted Kyle on the arm. "So. How is everyone?" he asked, carrying the wooden salad bowl to the middle of the table.

"Psyched," Josh said immediately.

"Oh yeah?" Nicole asked. "And why is that?"

Josh was the first to spoon enchiladas onto his plate. He took heaping bites, the orange cheese dripping from his fork. "Monster Mash," he said, talking with his mouth full. "It's this Saturday. Biggest party of the year."

Nicole raised her eyebrows. "I can't believe it's that time of year again."

"It comes around fast," Stephen said.

"A girl asked Josh if he was going to the Monster Mash today," Kyle piped up.

"That's right," Josh said, puffing up his chest. "Samantha Jeffries."ZZYZXZZYZXZZYZXZZYZXZZYZXZZ YZXZZYZXZZYZXZZYZXZZYZXZZYZX

"Samantha Jeffries?" Lori made a skeeved-out don't-go-there face.

"What's wrong with her?" Nicole asked.

"Nothing's wrong with her," Josh said quickly. "She's superhot."

"I hear she's a little high maintenance," Lori said, picking at her salad.

"Well, she's a model," Josh retorted. "Models require extraspecial care."

"That's one way to put it." Lori smirked.

"I'm psyched Samantha's going to be there," Josh said. "I think I'm in love, dude."

Nicole and Stephen looked at Josh, alarmed. "Love's a pretty big emotion, Josh," Stephen said carefully. "Are you sure?"

"Sure, I'm sure," Josh said breezily.

Nicole took a sip of her wine. "I liked it better when you guys were still trick-or-treating instead of going to parties. Remember when they were really little, Stephen? I used to dress them up as the same thing and you'd take them all over the neighborhood?"

"I'm happy those days are over," Stephen said with a mock groan. "It was always, 'One more house! One more house!' And remember how wired they used to get from all that candy?"

"Yeah, Mom, and don't remind us that you used to dress us the same." Lori made a face. "The worst was when you made us be crayons."

"You looked cute!" Nicole protested.

"When was that?" Josh asked, creasing his brow. "I don't remember that."

"You were only three," Lori pointed out. "Be thankful that it didn't scar your memory. You made them with that horrible itchy fabric, Mom. It was like *burlap* or something. It gave me a rash, remember? I was the red crayon, and by the end of the night, my face was all blotchy and red, too!"

"I spent a long time sewing those crayon costumes," Nicole huffed. "I have such cute pictures of you in them!"

Lori groaned. "*Please* do not get out the photo albums. I'm not sure I can survive another stroll down Halloween memory lane."

"Remember when you just *had* to be a pineapple, Lori?" Nicole asked. "A pineapple, of all things! I had the worst time figuring out how to make that costume."

"That costume was lame," Josh said with a laugh, then sipped his milk.

Lori shot him a look. "Remember when you wanted to be Pocahontas? You didn't quite realize she was a *girl*?"

"Oh, that was precious, Josh," Nicole cooed.

Josh shut his mouth and stared at his plate. "Okay. Enough."

Kyle took a bite of enchilada. It was frustrating how Lori and Josh—and everyone else in the world, really—took their pasts for granted. They could laugh about it, wince over it, tease each other with it, but at least it was there. "I wonder what kinds of things I was for Halloween," he said softly.

The family fell silent. Nicole put her arm on Kyle's shoulder. Josh sat back and chewed thoughtfully. He couldn't imagine what it must be like not to have a memory, like Kyle. Josh had a lot of sucky memories—failing a zillion tests, getting shots at the doctor's, his great-aunt Iris kissing him and her garlic breath—but he had lots of awesome ones, too—going on water slides, playing capture the flag with his friends in the backyard, getting an XBox for his birthday. Perhaps Kyle's alien species had wiped his memory when he fell to planet Earth. It was too bad. Josh would love to hear what it was like to be a kid on an alien planet. Probably violent and cool.

"You know, maybe you can't remember your past because you're part of some sort of secret spy organization," Josh volunteered. "You're like that dude in Quasar Master IV. Someone erased your memory because you know dangerous things."

Stephen looked at Josh curiously. "What's Quasar Master? A movie?"

"No, a video game," Josh answered.

Nicole rolled her eyes. "Should've guessed."

Josh turned to Kyle. "And now maybe someone's after you to make sure some of your memory doesn't come back. Maybe it's your job to save the planet, but the evil forces are trying to prevent you from doing so." He sat back and crossed his arms. This was his best Kyle theory yet.

"Josh, stop it," Nicole said quickly. "You're not being very sensitive." She patted Kyle's hand. "Don't worry about it, Kyle," she said. "You're bound to recall something soon. We'll put together a costume for you that will beat anything you've been for Halloween in the past."

Kyle brightened. "Really?"

"That's a great idea," Lori piped up. "I can help."

"Thanks," Kyle said.

"Do you think you'll go to the Monster Mash, Kyle?" Nicole asked.

"I don't know if I'm going, but I'm helping with the decorations," Kyle answered, taking a bite of beans.

Josh wrinkled his nose. "Why are you doing something girly like that?"

Kyle shrugged. "Amanda asked me to."

"Aha," Lori teased, wiping her mouth with her napkin.

"What?" Kyle looked at her.

"Nothing," Lori said, a smirk on her face.

Kyle sat back in his chair, feeling a little paranoid. "Amanda's my friend," he said slowly.

"Of course she is," Lori lilted. "Does Charlie know you're helping her with the decorations?"

"I-I don't know," Kyle stammered. His mind started to spin. Was he doing something wrong?

"Lori, stop it," Nicole scolded. She turned to Kyle. "I think it's nice you're helping with the decorations. It's good to get involved."

Kyle didn't respond. Would Charlie be upset? Kyle didn't know Charlie very well, but he sensed something fake about him. Kyle swished his milk around in his mouth, wondering if he should call up Amanda and cancel. Only . . . he really didn't want to.

After dinner, all the Tragers carried their plates over to the sink. Then Lori clomped upstairs to her room, Nicole and Stephen retreated to the den, and Kyle and Josh, who were on cleanup duty, started filling the sink with soapy water.

Josh came up beside Kyle and tapped his arm. "So. Nice jump from that tree today, Spider-Man."

Kyle ran his hands under the faucet. He was wondering why everyone was talking about this. "It wasn't such a big deal."

Josh gave him a crooked smile. "So . . . what's your secret? Did you have a bungee cord attached to you or something? Special springy shoes? Can you teach me how to do it?"

"Do what?" Kyle asked. "Jump?"

"Jump that far, yeah," Josh answered, scrubbing the enchilada pan. He watched as Kyle's expression didn't change, then widened his eyes. "There *was* no trick, was there?"

Kyle shrugged. "I just jumped. It wasn't that far."

"Dude, it was like two stories!" Josh whispered excitedly. "You heard my mom—when normal people jump from up there, they break their legs!"

Kyle's eyebrows furrowed. The jump seemed easy. Like nothing.

Josh stacked the silverware in the drying rack. He sighed, drained the sink, and threw the used sponge near the faucet. He turned to face Kyle. "You really *are* crazy—you know that?"

Kyle smiled uneasily. He didn't know what to say. Why could he jump from that height unharmed when others couldn't?

Josh wiped his hands on the dish towel and took the stairs two at a time to his bedroom. He shut the door, sat on his bed, and reached into his bedside table drawer for his little black spiral-bound notebook. He had written REASONS KYLE IS AN ALIEN on the first page in big, block letters.

He flipped through the pages, pausing to read through the evidence thus far: *Gets every IQ question correct. Learns to swim in one day. Fixes Dad's computer in a millisecond.* When he got to the end of the list, he uncapped his pen and wrote, *Can jump from massive heights and not get hurt.* Then he clapped the notebook shut. That was enough Kyle anthropology for now.

Josh felt around in his bedside drawer for the clipping he'd found in this past weekend's newspaper. It was a color photo of Samantha Jeffries, modeling a pink polo shirt for a local boutique. Josh slumped back on his bed and looked at her for a while. Samantha's lips were plump and pink, her eyes sparkly and enticing, and her body . . . words couldn't *describe* her body. In just a couple short days, if all went well, Samantha and Josh would be together.

As long as he got all his football terminology right, anyway.

5. The Ball's in His Court

The next day, Lori and Hillary followed the rest of the gym class to the middle of the indoor volleyball court. Those who were happy to be in gym class—aka the boys—were already batting the volleyball back and forth across the net, diving exaggeratedly to make shots. Lori would much rather be anywhere else but here. Math class, even.

It didn't help that Declan was in her gym class, too. Lori saw him immediately—he was standing at the back of the court, dribbling the volleyball like it was a basketball. She gritted her teeth and looked away.

The gym teacher, Coach Hawthorne, blew his whistle and instructed everyone to sit down and start warm-up stretches. As they plopped to the shiny wood floor, Hillary poked Lori's arm. "So, have you asked anyone to the Monster Mash yet?"

Lori shook her head. "I told you. I'm not asking anyone. Someone has to ask me."

"You're being ridiculous," Hillary answered.

"How about you?" Lori challenged. "Who have *you* asked?"

"I'm still trying to decide who I want to go with," Hillary said quickly.

"Why don't we just go together?" Lori suggested in a small voice.

"It would be much more fun with dates," Hillary argued. There was a glimmer in her eye. "So did you find out if Kyle is going?"

Lori grabbed the toes of her sneakers and stretched over her legs. "Get this—he's helping Amanda with the decorations."

Hillary clutched her heart and rolled her eyes. "He must have it *bad* to agree to help her with the decorations." She swooned. "I wish *I* had a guy falling over me like that."

"That's exactly what I thought," Lori agreed. "Although I'm not sure if Kyle understands what helping Amanda will entail. That, like, he'll have to blow up girly balloons and run around looking for Halloween-themed flowers and pick out appropriate dance music and stuff. I don't think he's ever been to a Halloween party. Sometimes it seems like he grew up in a bubble."

Hillary got a feisty look on her face. "What's it like, living in the same house as him? Do you ever, like, walk in on him while he's in the shower?"

Lori slugged her. "Enough."

"What? He's so sexy. And he's not such a moron anymore, right? He's going to school now, just like everyone else."

"The guy sleeps in a *bathtub*, Hill."

Hillary giggled. "That's even sexier." She got an intrigued, far-off look on her face. Lori could tell she was imagining Kyle sleeping in his bathtub naked. *Gross.*

The coach blew his whistle again. "Pretzel stretch!" he shouted.

Everyone crossed their right legs over their bent left knees and twisted like a pretzel. Hillary nudged Lori, then leaned over to whisper, "Don't look now, but a certain perv is watching you."

Lori stiffened. She peeked from under her hair to the other side of the court. Sure enough, Declan was staring at her. When Lori met his eyes, Declan didn't look away. Her heart started to beat faster. "Ick," she whispered, trying to sound as disgusted as possible.

"Should I yell something at him?" Hillary asked. "Or how about I send him a nasty text message?" She whipped out her cell phone, which she'd stuffed inside her sock.

"I think you're the only one bringing a phone to gym class," Lori snapped. Hillary was so addicted to her phone, she never went anywhere without it. "By the time Declan got the message, it wouldn't make any sense."

The coach blew his whistle and everyone assembled on the volleyball court. Hillary and Lori stood next to each other in the second row of players. Declan was on the other team, whispering to Jeff Preston. When he bent over to tie his sneaker, his shirt rode up, showing off his sexy ab muscles. Lori tried not to drool.

"You *sure* you don't still like him?" Hillary murmured. "You're totally staring."

"I am not!" Lori hissed.

A boy on the other team served the ball. It soared right for Lori, but she didn't react. It landed with a thud at her feet. Hillary stared at it as if it were an asteroid.

"Girls!" Coach Hawthorne yelled. "Pay more attention to the game, less attention to talking!"

Someone at the back scooped up the volleyball and rolled it back to the other team. Lori glared at Hillary. "I was *not* staring at Declan."

Hillary smirked. "Yes, you were."

"I am very much over him," Lori stated firmly. "He's a perv—just like you said. End of story." She squared her shoulders. The worst thing she could do was tell bigmouthed Hillary the truth—Hillary would run over and immediately tell Declan. Lori would risk Declan breaking her heart all over again.

Hillary rocked back and forth on her heels. "So then, you probably don't care that he asked me about you," she said.

Lori looked at her carefully. The volleyball came whizzing toward her again, but luckily a player next to her stepped in and bopped the ball back over the net. "He was asking about me?" She tried to say it casually, adding a small yawn.

"Uh-huh." Hillary's blond ponytail bobbed up and down. "He asked if you were going with anyone to the Monster Mash."

Lori stared straight ahead. "Really?"

"Yep."

"And what did you say?"

"That you didn't have a date yet."

Lori's mouth fell open. She stamped her foot. "Hills! You should have told him I *did* have a date! Somebody really cute from another school that he hasn't met!"

"How was I supposed to know?" Hillary protested.

Lori gritted her teeth. Now Declan probably thought she was desperate and pathetic.

Hillary put her hand on Lori's shoulder. "Why don't you just talk to him? It's obvious you guys both still like each other."

Lori stared vacantly at the giant Beachwood High Regional Basketball Champs pennant on the other side of the gym. She felt a million things at once. Excited, giddy, anxious . . . but she couldn't show any of it. She pretended to be really into the volleyball game, clapping when someone made a point. Until she realized—

she was clapping for the *other team*. A few of her team-mates glared at her.

Hillary leaned in to say something else, when the volleyball whizzed right over their heads yet again. Coach Hawthorne blew his whistle, stopping play. He marched over to the girls. "Ms. Trager and Ms. Pierce, is there a problem?"

Hillary blinked. "Problem? Why?"

"Are you allergic to volleyball, perhaps?" the gym teacher said with a smirk. When neither girl answered, he sighed. "I'm separating you two. Lori, go over to the other team. Stand next to Mr. McDonough. Hillary, go to the back of the court. You're serving next."

"I'm serving?" Hillary squeaked. Lori knew for a fact that Hillary hated serving—she always hurt her hands and broke a nail. She always got people to switch with her so she never had to.

But Lori thought she'd really gotten the raw end of the deal. She ducked under the net and wove around the players. Declan watched her as she approached, a wisp of a smile on his chiseled face. He stepped aside and made a space next to him. Lori tried not to note how muscular his legs looked in his baggy red gym shorts. How come guys looked awesome in whatever they wore, even polyester gym shorts and a ratty cotton T-shirt? Lori pushed a few stray strands of hair behind her ears and hoped she hadn't eaten off all her lip gloss.

"Hey, Trager," Declan said as Lori stiffly took her place beside him.

"Hey, McDonough," Lori answered in her best I'm-cool-with-everything voice.

Declan gave her a knowing look. "You needed an excuse to talk to me, so you got yourself separated from Hillary over to our team, huh?"

Lori's mouth dropped open. *"No!"*

"It was just a joke," Declan said quietly. "You don't have to sound so offended."

Lori sulkily crossed her arms over her chest and shut her eyes. "Sorry."

Hillary served. The ball careened off the court. Hillary let out a high-pitched wail and immediately started sucking on her left index finger.

"So how've you been?" Declan asked.

"Fine," Lori said crisply. "Good. Perfect."

Declan nodded. "Glad to hear it." He stepped forward to spike the ball over the net. Lori watched him from behind. She'd forgotten how effortlessly he moved. It made her ache a little; it was incredible that not long ago, they had been hanging out every day.

"So what's new in your life?" Declan asked, moving back into position. "I haven't talked to you in a while."

Lori rolled her eyes. How long were they going to have this awkward conversation? "Same old crap, different day. You?"

"Yeah, sounds about right," Declan answered.

The ball soared back to them again. It flew straight for Lori's head. She clasped her arms together but knew she wasn't going to be able to hit the volleyball remotely hard enough to send it back over the net. Her limbs froze. Suddenly Declan shot in front of her, bumping the ball out of Lori's way. Lori stepped forward at the same time, and they collided. Lori felt herself start to fall, but then Declan's strong arms scooped her up. For a second, they were pressed together. Declan's skin smelled like the lemony soap he always used. His skin was soft, and she could feel his flexed biceps through his T-shirt. She was sure he could feel how fast her heart was beating.

They broke away. Declan had a sheepish little smile on his face. Lori didn't know where to look. "Sorry," Declan said.

"It's cool," Lori answered, straightening up. "Thanks for . . . you know. Playing my position. The ball was coming straight for my head. I probably would've gotten brain damage if it hit me."

Declan smiled coyly. "And we can't have that, can we, Trager?"

Lori fluttered her eyelashes flirtatiously. "Of course not."

When she looked in his deep brown eyes, she wondered if all her insecurities were stupid. Maybe things would be okay between them. Maybe Declan really did ask Hillary if Lori had a date for the Mash because he liked her. She took a deep breath. "So . . . um, are you going to the Monster Mash?" she blurted out.

Declan raised an eyebrow. "Probably. You?"

"Maybe," Lori said, pursing her lips and swaying back and forth. "You going with anyone?"

"I was just going to go by myself," Declan answered.

A few agonizing seconds passed. A terrible taste filled Lori's mouth. Surely, Declan would say the simple magic words—*Unless . . . you want to go with me?*—any minute now. But Declan continued to just stand there. What, was he expecting *her* to say something? *Maybe I* should *ask him*, Lori thought. Maybe Hillary was right.

Then a horrible feeling struck her. What if she asked Declan and he said no? What if he *laughed*? Perhaps he really had asked Hillary if Lori was taking a date for a completely different reason. Or perhaps Hillary was lying—maybe Declan hadn't asked her anything at all. That was most likely it. Hillary was probably just trying to bolster Lori's confidence.

"Well, Declan, good luck finding a date," she said bitterly, sticking her nose up into the air. An acid, searing feeling shot through her stomach.

Declan scratched his head. "Huh?" He looked confused. "Wait. I just said I was going alone."

"Do you mind?" Lori snapped, her eye on the other team. "I'm trying to play volleyball."

Declan had a baffled look on his face. "I totally don't get you, Trager. One minute, you're all nice and normal, and the next . . . you're being all—" He waved his hands around, perhaps to indicate *crazy*.

Lori clenched her teeth. How dare Declan try to turn this around to be about her! Didn't he realize why she was acting weird? Was it so hard to just *ask* her out? "I'm not being all *anything*," she said sharply. "I'm fine. Really."

But she felt a wobbly, prickly heat rising into her face. She knew that in a few seconds, she was going to start crying. She bolted from her spot, grabbed the wooden bathroom pass on the bleachers, and marched into the locker room. She banged into a stall, sat down on the toilet, and put her head in her hands. She had a feeling she'd be staying just like this for the rest of the period. Maybe even the rest of the day.

6. The Secret Language of Girls

little bit later that same day, Kyle picked up his lunch tray and gazed around the cafeteria. The whole place was abuzz with laugher, shouting, and gossiping. There was a huge line of kids to get pizza, soft pretzels, and little cups of ice cream; and the whole room smelled like French fries and whatever lemony stuff the custodians used to clean the tables and floors. Different groups sat in different areas: the skaters near the graffiti wall, the cheerleaders and jocks in the center of the cafeteria where everyone could see them, the math nerds off to the side where everyone *couldn't* see them. Kyle wondered if things were like this at his old school, wherever his old school was. Did every school have distinct groups, with their marked cafeteria territories? Where would the old Kyle have sat?

"Kyle!" a girl's voice called out. Kyle looked over. Hillary and Lori were sitting at a table nearby. "Over here!" Hillary called.

Kyle sat down next to them. "Hey, guys."

"You were looking a little lost there," Hillary said, putting the cap back on her tube of lipstick. Hillary liked to look made-up, even while she ate.

"Yeah, you were standing there like a zombie," Lori seconded, adjusting the sleeve on her white polo shirt.

"I was just taking it all in," Kyle explained.

"Taking all of *what* in?" Hillary asked.

"High school," Kyle said quietly. "Lunch. I don't know."

Lori pointed a carrot stick at him. "You're acting like you've never been to high school before."

Kyle shrugged. He kind of hadn't been.

Hillary put her soda straw in her mouth and sucked. "You're making the cutest face right now. Like a little lost duckling."

Kyle slowly opened his lunch bag, his cheeks burning. Okay, so standing in the cafeteria looking around was apparently weird. He added it to the ever-growing list of Things He Shouldn't Do in School—things he didn't necessarily understand but nevertheless had to remember. Sometimes the rules were awfully hard to keep track of. He always had to keep moving in the halls, for instance, unless he saw someone he knew. Then he could stop and talk. It wasn't appropriate to talk to someone he *didn't* know, however, and it definitely wasn't appropriate to interrupt a couple making out. And two days ago, when Kyle and Mr. Miller, his math teacher, had been strolling down the hall discussing quadratic equations, Josh had pulled Kyle aside, hissing "Abort mission! Abort mission! Hasn't anyone told you it's social death to talk with teachers *outside* class?" Kyle had to add that rule to his list, too.

"Hey!" a voice said above them. Kyle looked up just in time to see Amanda sitting down next to Lori. His heart started beating faster. "Do you guys mind if I sit here?" Amanda asked.

"Sure," Hillary said.

"No problem," Lori seconded.

Amanda pulled the foil off her sandwich. She turned to Kyle and gave him a friendly smile. "So, Kyle, are your lips in good shape?"

Kyle froze. The packet of Sour Patch Kids fell out of his hand. "I'm . . . sorry?"

Hillary giggled behind her hand.

Amanda had a very businesslike look on her face. "We have about two hundred balloons to blow up this afternoon for the Monster Mash," she explained. She looked at Hillary and Lori. "Kyle's helping me with the decorations this year."

"So we've heard," Lori said.

"Do you guys want to help, too?" Amanda asked them.

"No thanks." Hillary smirked. "I don't want to waste my lip power on blowing up balloons."

"She wants to save her lips for things we won't mention at this table." Lori rolled her eyes and nudged her.

Kyle looked back and forth at Hillary and Lori. Sometimes the two of them seemed to speak in a different language, one that involved a lot of eyebrow lifts, half sentences, and giggles. Kyle might have learned the contents of the school library's entire set of encyclopedias and a couple of foreign languages in a single day, but he was backward when it came to girls.

"Thanks anyway, though," Hillary said to Amanda. "I'm sure the decorations are going to rock. How's the work going on the haunted house?"

"I don't know," Amanda answered. "That's the guys' territory. But they say it's going to be really scary."

Lori shivered. "I freaked in the haunted house last year. I'm not sure if I want to go through that again."

"Lori scares easily," Hillary pointed out.

"Shut *up*," Lori said, nudging Hillary again. "Speaking of scary, apparently my brother has a major crush on Samantha Jeffries." She looked around the table, raising her eyebrows.

Hillary crunched on a potato chip. "Yikes."

Kyle looked at Lori curiously. "What's wrong with Samantha?"

Lori raised one shoulder. "I heard she was one of those crazy girlfriends. Superdemanding. Guys that date her are totally whipped."

"I don't understand girls like that," Amanda mused, sipping from her juice box. "I mean, what's the point of ordering someone around like that? I would just feel terrible."

"That's because you're so nice," Hillary lilted.

"I guess," Amanda said, shrugging. She turned back to Kyle, shooting him a warm, sweet smile. "Well, anyway, I'm glad you're going to help with the decorations, Kyle." Her eyes crinkled adorably. "And I'll try not to order *you* around."

"Not that you're his girlfriend, anyway," Hillary pointed out.

Kyle's mouth fell open. Amanda's eyes widened. She let out a nervous laugh. "Well, no. That's not what I meant, of course . . ."

"Of course you didn't," Kyle said quickly, certain his whole face was beet red with embarrassment.

"Amanda!" a voice interrupted them. Kyle looked up. Charlie Tanner crossed the room toward them. He was over six feet tall, with dark, spiky hair; broad shoulders; and a lazy, self-satisfied smile. He reached them quickly, clapping his hand on Amanda's shoulder. Amanda jumped up and spun around.

"Hi!" she chirped. "Where have you been? I was looking for you!"

"I was right over there." Charlie pointed to a bunch

of basketball players sitting at a corner table. Like Charlie, they were all tall, good-looking, and well dressed. He glanced around at the table. "Mind if I steal her away? We have secret Monster Mash stuff to discuss."

"Charlie's working on the haunted house," Amanda explained quickly. She looked at Charlie. "Kyle's going to help me with the decorations this afternoon, since you stole all my workers."

Charlie raised an eyebrow. His expression twitched for a moment, then settled. "Oh. Well. That's cool."

"Is something wrong?" Amanda sounded uncertain.

"Nothing at all." Charlie sounded distracted. "Let's go."

Amanda glanced at Lori, Hillary, and Kyle. "See you guys." She and Charlie strode away, holding hands. Charlie whispered something to Amanda that none of them could hear. Amanda glanced over her shoulder, staring straight at Kyle. Then she said something back to Charlie. There was a defensive look on her face.

"I hear Charlie keeps her on a short leash," Hillary murmured. "I hear he's jealous of everyone."

"You keep saying that," Lori pointed out. "But where are you hearing it from?"

"I told you, I don't remember," Hillary remarked. She stared at Charlie. "He sure is cute, though."

"You think *everyone's* cute," Lori complained.

Kyle watched Amanda and Charlie disappear out the cafeteria door, wishing *he* were the one holding Amanda's hand. He cleared his throat and stared down at his lunch: a peanut butter sandwich, sour cream and onion potato chips, and Sour Patch Kids. Without

Amanda here, he suddenly didn't feel hungry anymore. He noticed Lori staring at him. Then Hillary. They exchanged a look and then started staring at him again. "What?" Kyle asked.

"Poor, poor Kyle," Hillary murmured quietly.

"You've got it bad, huh?" Lori simpered.

"Got what bad?" Kyle asked defensively, crushing his paper napkin in his hands.

"You can admit you like her, Kyle," Lori said quietly. "It's just us. We won't tell."

Kyle bit his lip, not answering. *Was it really that obvious?*

Hillary leaned forward on her elbows. "I think she likes you, too, Kyle. But she probably doesn't want to take the risk."

Kyle frowned. "What do you mean?"

Lori took a sip of her soda. "What Hillary means is that you're new to this school, and girls don't want to take a chance on an unknown guy. They want to know that *other* girls like the guy, too—not just them. If you want Amanda to like you, Amanda has to think you're in demand."

Kyle stared at both of them. "So how do I make Amanda realize that I'm . . . I'm in demand?"

"I have an idea." Hillary snaked her arm around Kyle's shoulders. "Take me to the Monster Mash. Once Amanda sees you've got a date, she'll realize how badly she wants you." Kyle stared at Hillary as he slowly took a bite of his sandwich.

"*Hillary*, no," Lori warned in the same voice she might use to discipline a dog. "Not a good idea."

Hillary widened her eyes innocently. "What? We'd just go as friends. It will be a *ruse*. And it's for a good cause, right? You and Amanda would look so cute together. You two goody-goodies deserve each other."

Lori creased her empty chip bag back and forth, feeling torn. Hillary had been all over Kyle at Jeff's party. Kyle was absolutely no match for a girl like her. Lori wasn't sure if she could allow this to happen in good conscience. "You can only go as friends," Lori warned. She looked at Kyle. "Okay, Kyle? Don't let her hang on you the whole time."

Hillary's eyebrows angled into a V. "Lori, if we act all buddy-buddy, it won't have an impact. I have to be a *little* all over Kyle to get the point across."

Lori clenched her teeth. She looked at Kyle. "What do *you* think about all this?"

"I don't know," Kyle said slowly. "What if Amanda sees me with Hillary and just thinks we're . . . together? And doesn't care?"

Hillary patted Kyle's shoulder. "You are just *precious*, Kyle! So young and naive!" She sat back. "Believe me, Amanda *will* care. Tell you what. How about I give you a crash course on the ins and outs of winning a girl and making her jealous? There are tons of things I could teach you. And when we're done, I guarantee Amanda will be throwing rocks at your window at night, begging to be with you."

Kyle frowned. "Amanda wouldn't throw rocks at my window. She's not destructive."

Hillary rolled her eyes. "It's an *expression*."

Kyle looked at Lori. "I don't know . . ."

Lori sighed. "I have to say, Hillary's methods would probably work. She's a pro at game playing. The best in the business."

"Yes, and if *you'd* heed some of my game-playing tactics, maybe you'd have your Monster Mash dream date, too." Hillary winked at Lori.

Lori bristled. "That's quite enough."

"What's she talking about?" Kyle asked.

"Nothing," Lori said quickly.

Hillary looked at Kyle. "Lori likes a guy. Except she's too scared to ask him because of some . . . baggage between the two of them."

Lori slugged Hillary on the arm. "Just butt out, okay? It's none of your business!"

Kyle had a feeling he should change the subject before the two of them got in a fight. "But why do people have to play games at all?" he asked. "I mean, why do I have to pretend to be with you, Hillary? Why can't I just be honest with Amanda?"

Lori burst out laughing. Hillary laid her head on Kyle's shoulder. "You're so sweet, Kyle." The bell rang, and she scrunched her lunch bag and stood up. Hillary plucked a pink leather day planner out of her bag and flipped forward a few pages. "How about we have our first lesson tomorrow? We'll call it Operation Make Her Jealous. How about it?"

"I think I'll pass," Kyle said quietly.

"You'll change your mind," Hillary said lightly, looping her white suede bag over her shoulder and walking away. "Believe me, by the day's end, you're going to beg me for my help. I totally guarantee it."

The rest of the students filed out of the cafeteria, too. Kyle stared at his half-eaten lunch, a tight, swirling feeling in his stomach. He didn't know what to think. On one hand, he really, *really* wanted Amanda to like him. But on the other, he hated the idea of doing it dishonestly.

Only, maybe Hillary was right. Maybe *all* girls functioned like this—maybe they all responded to the same things. Kyle shut his eyes and put his thumbs to his temples. Once again, he wished his memory hadn't been stolen away from him. In his past life, he probably knew all these rules and behaviors. He was probably as comfortable in high school and with girls as everyone else seemed to be. If only he could get some of his memory back. Learning about this stuff wasn't as easy as digesting encyclopedias or appreciating the beauty of math—it took *work*.

When he opened his eyes, a crawling feeling came over him. It was the same feeling he'd had yesterday—the feeling that someone was watching.

Kyle looked around. The cafeteria was empty. In the kitchen, the cafeteria workers scrubbed away at the dirty pots. A fluorescent overhead light in the corner flickered. A breeze from one of the open windows made the edges of the nutrition posters on the far walls flutter.

I'm probably jumpy because of that episode in the yard yesterday, Kyle rationalized. He slid his hand in his pocket and felt for the key fob. It was there, as it had been all morning. He was still trying to decide what to do with it. Part of him was curious what it accessed—someone's e-mail? Important information? Would he ever know? Did it matter?

Slowly, he got to his feet and crumpled up his lunch bag into a ball, the remnants of his sandwich still inside. He noticed a blue plastic trash can at the other side of the cafeteria. Could he make it? He raised the bag above his head and let go. The bag flew through the air in a high, perfect arc and landed square in the trash can. Kyle stood back, satisfied. At least he did *one* thing right today.

All the cars in the cafeteria parking lot were empty. All

of them, that was, save one—a battered white pickup truck. The inside of the truck smelled like cigarettes and stale coffee, and the radio was set to a local Seattle news channel. Tom Foss sat in the driver's seat, holding a pair of expensive binoculars to his face. He watched as Kyle tossed his lunch bag into the trash can across the cafeteria and strode slowly out of room into the outdoor corridor.

Foss brought his cell phone back to his ear and heard the person on the other end cough. "So he was showing off his powers?" the voice asked.

"Yes," Foss answered, thinking of Kyle's miraculous two-story jump from the tree house yesterday. "And they're starting to get . . . noticed."

"We have to put a stop to this," the voice on the other end said smoothly, "before it's too late. Can you handle it?"

"Of course," Foss answered. He watched as Kyle joined a stream of students in the hall. Kyle already looked like he fit in at Beachwood High—but that was impossible. Kyle would never fit in here. Or anywhere. Which was what was so dangerous about him being out in the world. "I'm on it," Foss added.

"Good," the voice said.

Foss hung up the phone and slid it back into his briefcase. He slumped against the truck's worn leather seat. Then he felt around in his jeans pocket, looking for something. He frowned. It was missing. He tried the other pocket. Not there either. Panicked, he stuck his hands into the compartments of his briefcase, then into the bottom of the bag, then into the cupholders of the car. Nothing. He bent down and searched beneath the seats. After a few minutes, he sat back up, beads of sweat dotting his forehead. This didn't make any sense.

Foss started up the truck and backed out of the parking space. As he paused at the stop sign to turn out into the road, he banged his fist on the steering wheel, pulled out his cell phone, and hit the redial button.

The same voice answered. "What is it now?" he asked.

Foss felt nervous. "It's gone," he said sheepishly.

"What's gone?"

"The fob."

There was a long silence. Foss stared anxiously at the truck's odometer and mileage gauge. "*How?*" the voice finally replied.

"I don't know. It's just . . . not here. I've looked all over the truck."

"And what about at the . . . room?"

Foss shut his eyes, thinking. "Absolutely not. I didn't need it last night. The last time I can remember having it is . . ." A lump formed in his throat. "When I was in the yard, watching Kyle. Yesterday."

"Could you have dropped it?" the voice asked, growing annoyed.

"Of course not!" Foss growled. But then he stopped. He thought about how he'd frantically run from the Trager yard yesterday when he thought Kyle had seen him. *Had* he dropped it?

"I don't know," he said weakly.

"Well, you'd better find it," the voice hissed. "You know what would happen if it fell into the wrong hands."

Foss pulled the truck around the long winding driveway leading away from the school and glanced through the windows again. Kyle was now walking down the corridor to his next class. One hand swung at his side, but the other was snug in his pocket, as if he were holding something. *Was it possible?*

Foss straightened up. "I'm going to have to go back on their property."

"Fine. Do whatever you have to do," the voice said sinisterly. "Just *get it back*."

Foss clapped his phone shut and put the truck into drive again. He had his orders. If Kyle had what Foss thought he had, Foss would have to stop at nothing to get it back. *Nothing*.

7. Step by Step

Tuesday afternoon, Kyle stood in the middle of the Beachwood Rec Center, a giant, airy, ballroom overlooking the Puget Sound on one side and the Johnson Memorial Cemetery on the other—which made it the perfect setting for a Halloween party. Earlier, he and Amanda had blown up one hundred orange and black balloons, which now bobbed gently at their feet. They'd also hung fake spiderwebs around all the windows and put fake rats, spiders, scorpions, and bats all over the doorways. Kyle had climbed up to some of the lower light fixtures and installed black lights, which were supposed to make everything glow eerily in the dark. Now Amanda stood up on a ladder, pushing a paint roller over the ballroom's far wall. The rec center had decided to allow them to paint a giant Halloween graveyard mural, as long as they painted over it after the party. So far, Kyle and Amanda had painted the sky black and the grass green, and they still had to fill in the headstones; ghosts; vampires; hAowling coDyotes; Aand the full, eMerie moon. SomBe of the pAaints weYre oils, anLd Kyle wIas getting a littlNe woozy from the smell of the turpentine they were using to clean the brushes.

"God, I'm getting so exhausted." Amanda lowered her arm and shook it out. "My arm feels like it might drop off. Although . . . a severed arm would make a great prop for the party."

"I'm tired, too," Kyle lied. In truth, he felt as

energetic as he had when he came in. Amanda's eyes had widened as she'd watched Kyle blow up balloon after balloon, hardly even catching his breath in between. Kyle wondered if it was weird to be able to blow up so many balloons so easily—just like it was weird to jump to the ground from the tree house and not be hurt.

Amanda climbed down off the ladder and stood back, appraising the mural. "It's getting there," she said slowly. "Ready to start on the moon?"

"Sure," Kyle answered. He glanced at Amanda out of the corner of his eye. She looked so beautiful. She wore a soft white sweater, and a blue ribbon held her long, blond hair away from her face. She rolled the brush over the wall with the same upright, elegant posture she had when she was playing the piano.

"Thanks so much for helping," Amanda said again. "I could never have done all this by myself."

"Sure," Kyle said. He picked up a clean brush, dipped it into some yellow paint, and climbed the ladder to fill in the moon. "But why did you take on all this work to start with? Why didn't you get a whole new committee of people a long time ago?"

"I should have, I know," Amanda said, "but I thought I could handle it myself. I'm like that sometimes—I take on things that are way over my head. Maybe it's so I can prove to myself I can do it. Or maybe working by myself means I have complete control over it. I don't know." She glanced at Kyle and bit her lip. "Although . . . I'm sort of glad that I didn't have a committee and it's just you working with me."

"Really?" Kyle asked. He didn't dare look away from his moon painting, for fear his eyes would give everything away.

"It's fun hanging out with you," Amanda said. "This is like secret Kyle and Amanda time, you know?"

Kyle felt himself blushing. He pressed his paintbrush into the wall. Excess paint squeezed out, instantly dripping down the wall. "Oops."

"It's cool." Amanda rushed for a big roll of paper towels and started blotting up the dripping paint. She giggled. "Actually, it looks good. Like the moon is bleeding. *Very* Halloween."

Kyle laughed shakily. "So . . . it seems like you really like Halloween."

"I guess," Amanda answered. "Doesn't everyone?"

"I don't know." Kyle thought for a moment. "It's funny. Josh had to explain to me what Halloween was. And, to be honest, I think it's kind of odd."

"Odd? How so?"

Kyle paused. He liked how Amanda didn't make fun of him for not knowing what Halloween was, like Josh did. She never judged him. "Well, it's odd that people want to dress up as someone else," Kyle explained. "It sort of seems like lying."

Amanda swished her black-coated brush in their bucket of water, cleaning it off. "I don't think it's lying. Halloween is supposed to be fun, not serious. And what's so wrong with pretending to be someone else for a little while? There are lots of times I'd much rather be, I don't know, Catwoman instead of Amanda Bloom."

Kyle laughed and shrugged. "I guess it's kind of hard being me, too."

Amanda started filling in a gray headstone, swiping her brush back and forth against the wall. "I would think it would be pretty cool being you. You're super-awesome at math. I wish I were."

"But I have no memory," Kyle pointed out. "I can't remember my parents. My past."

Amanda pursed her lips. A sad look came over her face. "I know. That's got to be hard. But I sometimes wish I didn't remember my past, either. Then it wouldn't hurt so much."

"Are you thinking about your dad?" Kyle asked.

"Yeah," Amanda said softly. "I really miss him around Halloween. He used to love it." She smiled, thinking. "He loved making costumes for me. When I was in fourth grade, he made me a Mr. Peanut costume. It was this giant peanut structure with a big papier-mâché top hat. It sounds crazy, but it was so cool. I had big shoes and a cane, too, and everyone at school loved it. I even won a prize in the school's Halloween costume contest. I gave the ribbon to my dad. I was so proud of him."

"That's great," Kyle said softly.

"The first year he got really sick, he was in the hospital over Halloween and wasn't able to make me a costume," Amanda went on. "I just had to buy something. It was this ugly, generic superhero costume, and I hated it. I didn't even want to go trick-or-treating. But my dad told me that it didn't matter—on Halloween, magical things happened. All reality is suspended. You really *become* the character you're dressed up as—and he said I would really turn into a superhero." She put down her brush and got a far-off look in her eyes. "I was so convinced I would be . . . powerful. I thought maybe I would gain magical powers and cure him."

"That makes sense," Kyle said.

Amanda shrugged. "It didn't work, of course. My dad didn't get better after that night. But I *still* felt pretty magical."

"Really?" Kyle asked.

Amanda gave him a teasing look. "I got tons of candy." She and Kyle giggled for a moment. "But to answer your question, I don't think it's lying to dress up as someone else on Halloween. I think my dad was right—on Halloween, rules are suspended. Anything goes. You can pretend to be whomever you want. You can hide who you really are and instead be whomever or whatever you want to be. And that's okay."

"I didn't think about it that way," Kyle said slowly. He finished the last stroke of the moon and climbed down from the ladder.

Amanda turned back to the mural. "Hey, this is looking good." They'd finished the entire sky. The mural stretched dramatically from one end of the ballroom to the other.

"I guess we're a good team," Kyle said.

"It looks that way," Amanda said back.

They heard bursts of laughter and turned around. Two tall boys in black polo shirts, dark jeans, and sneakers came through the front entrance. "Hey, Amanda," one of them called. The other waved.

"Hi," Amanda said back. She and Kyle watched as the boys wandered over to the brown clapboard house in the corner. The house had worn, weathered roof shingles and blacked-out, asymmetrical windows. Amanda had draped tons of spiderweb gauze all over the porch railings and around the doors.

"That's the haunted house," Amanda whispered, following Kyle's gaze. "And those are the guys who were *supposed* to be on my decorations committee but ditched me to work on it instead."

"What's a haunted house?" Kyle asked slowly.

Amanda smiled. "Seriously? You don't know?"

Kyle shrugged. "I guess I can assume it's a house that's . . . haunted?"

"Bingo!" Amanda cried. "You get a gold pumpkin sticker." She peeled off one from a strip of stickers they'd used on one of the Monster Mash posters in the rec center hallway and pressed it to Kyle's chest.

"Only . . . what does *haunted* mean?" Kyle asked.

"Well, it means that it's overrun by ghosts," Amanda explained. "Like, if someone died in the house, he could come back and roam around it as a ghost. And make noises and moan and freak out the people that live there now. So he haunts it."

"Ah," Kyle said.

"In last year's haunted house, ghosts were floating around everywhere."

Kyle frowned. "For real?"

"No, of course not," Amanda said. "They used trick mirrors or something. I don't know. The guys always try to make it scarier than the year before. Only seniors can work on it, and it's like a macho class kind of thing." She bent down and uncapped a can of orange paint. "This year, I hear they're using some sort of mechanical devices to get corpses and stuff to spring out of chairs and move across the floor."

"How do you know?" Kyle asked.

Amanda straightened up. Her eyes darted back and forth. "Charlie's on the committee. He told me."

"Oh," Kyle said.

They both looked away. It felt like an unhappy spirit had just invaded the room. It was the first time Amanda had mentioned Charlie this afternoon. Kyle thought about Amanda's distressed expression when Charlie had shown up at lunch. And about what Hillary had said at lunch—that Charlie was jealous of everyone and kept Amanda on a short leash. Was that true? Was Amanda not talking about Charlie for a reason?

"I don't know if I've ever been to a haunted house," Kyle said, changing the subject, "or to a big party like this." He stared past the guys and the haunted house to the platform stage at the end of the room. There were a bunch of speakers in the back and a few microphones sitting in the center. Amanda had told him that a band would be playing at the Mash. "I don't even know if I've ever danced."

"Come on," Amanda said. "I bet you have."

Kyle shrugged. "If I have, I've forgotten how."

Amanda took a few steps toward him. "There's nothing to it." She glanced over toward the haunted house. The boys had ducked inside. "Do you want me to give you a lesson?"

Kyle pushed one hand deep in his pocket. He had never danced before.

Amanda smiled. "Just a quick one. I'll show you all the basics."

Kyle chewed on his lip. "Well . . ."

But before he knew it, Amanda had taken his left hand and put her left hand on his right shoulder. Her hands felt soft and small. There were speckles of paint on her palms and under her fingernails. "You move to the left, like this, and then put your feet together, and then move to the back, and together, and then to the right, together, and to the front, together."

She guided Kyle through the movements. After a couple rounds, Kyle got it. "That's kind of a formal style of dancing," Amanda explained. "Most kids just sort of sway back and forth." She demonstrated, stepping from side to side without moving back. Kyle tried to follow her, but stomped on her feet a couple of times.

"But then there's another way to dance for people who really like each other," Amanda said in a slow voice. "You want to see what that's like?"

Kyle swallowed hard. He was afraid to answer. Amanda threw her arms around his neck. She moved her body close, pressing her waist up against his. She laid her head in the crook of his neck. Kyle felt his limbs slowly freeze. He tried not to think about how Amanda smelled deliciously like honeysuckle. How her hair tickled his chin. How Amanda's head seemed so natural on his chest, like it fit. He tried not to think about anything, and stared fixedly at the linoleum floor.

"Wrap your arms around my waist," Amanda instructed. Kyle did, touching her very, very lightly. He felt how tiny Amanda's waist was. He could probably pick her up and spin her around.

"And you sway like this," Amanda said, dragging him back and forth. "Slowly, though. It's supposed to be romantic."

Kyle felt like he was going to burst. It felt like little bolts of lightning were flying back and forth under his skin. He was so close to Amanda's face. Would it be terrible to lean down, right now, and kiss her? He stared at the curled snail shell of her ear. Suddenly she looked up and met his eyes. She smiled . . . and leaned forward. Kyle's heart thumped wildly. He leaned forward, too.

"Look out!" someone screamed.

He and Amanda turned around. One of the beams that held up the haunted house's porch suddenly cracked and splintered off. Then, the roof buckled. Someone screamed. A wall fell down, kicking up a huge cloud of dust.

"Oh my God," Amanda whispered. The smoke cleared, and all the guys sauntered out, laughing. Including Charlie. "I'm okay, I'm okay," he said to everyone around him. He saw Amanda across the ballroom. "Hey!" he cried, starting over to them.

Amanda's skin turned a few shades paler. She immediately dropped Kyle's hand. "Charlie," she said in a tiny voice. "I didn't know you were coming today." Pink splotches began to form on her cheeks.

"Yeah, I was able to make it after all," Charlie said. He reached Amanda and swooped her up in her arms. Amanda whooped and giggled. After Charlie set her down, his eyes landed on Kyle.

"Hey there," he said gruffly to Kyle. He turned back to Amanda. "Putting him to work, like you said? Are you making him hang those lights you couldn't reach?"

Kyle could see Amanda's throat bob up and down as she swallowed. "Uh-huh," she said. She didn't look in Kyle's direction at all. "We're done for the day, though."

"Great," Charlie said. He grabbed Amanda's wrist. "Want a sneak peek at the haunted house?"

"Sure!" Amanda cried. She reached up and pecked Charlie on the cheek, and then they started across the ballroom without even saying good-bye. Kyle stood there, watching Amanda's bouncy walk. She didn't turn around and look at him once. He felt like she had taken his heart in her hands and twisted hard.

Kyle put a roll of crepe paper back in Amanda's cardboard box of supplies, trying to ignore the sounds of Amanda and Charlie laughing across the room. The only trouble was, Kyle could still smell Amanda's honeysuckle perfume on his neck. He could still feel his arms around her waist. But maybe what had just happened—their magical slow dance—had all been in his imagination.

8. Zero Tolerance

Tuesday night, Josh stared at his flickering computer screen, narrowing his eyes at the little alien spaceships in his scope. "Gotcha," he whispered, annihilating one. It exploded into nothingness. "You can run, but you can't hide."

"Josh?" His mom poked her head into the room. She was dressed in a black beaded sweater, black dressy pants, and fancy pointed-toe shoes. A swirl of fruity perfume wafted around her. Josh jumped, quickly minimized the game, and clicked over to the Word document he had open. He shuffled the papers on his desk and opened his history book on his lap to make it look like he'd been working.

"I just wanted to tell you that Dad and I are leaving soon," his mom said. Josh's parents were going out to dinner tonight alone—a rarity for them. "Are you sure you'll be okay here without Lori? I could call her at Hillary's house and tell her to come home."

"Mom, I'm *fifteen*." Josh sat up taller. "Cut the cord a little, will you? I'm probably going to be at the computer all night, doing my homework."

"How's the history report going?" she asked, sitting down on his bed.

"Good," Josh answered, turning back around to face his computer. "Really coming along."

His mom leaned over Josh's shoulder. She frowned. "You've only written three sentences. Isn't it supposed to be four pages long?"

Suddenly, a digitized explosion burbled out of the computer speakers. *"Game over, mere mortal,"* a satanic voice boomed. Josh winced. He'd forgotten to turn off the game's sound.

His mother cleared her throat. "I was just playing for *two* seconds," Josh said. "I needed to clear my mind. Prepare myself for my paper."

His mom sighed. "Maybe Dad and I should stay home and watch you. So you actually do your paper instead of kill aliens."

Josh rolled his eyes. "I'm going to do it, okay?" The last thing he wanted was a babysitter in his room all night. His parents never let him have any fun. It was all, *do your homework, do your chores, don't watch TV, don't play video games*. They had put parental controls on his computer. Even the Victoria's Secret site was blocked. "And, anyway, chill. It's not due until next Friday."

His mother shut her large blue eyes. "I'm worried about Kyle, too. He's seemed a little distracted lately. Do you think he'll be okay here alone? Maybe I should call a babysitter."

"Mom," Josh said sharply, "there are *two* of us here. If people at school find out I had a babysitter, I won't be able to show my face for years."

"Okay," his mother said uncertainly. She walked out of the room. Josh waited until he was sure she had walked down all eleven steps to the first floor, then he brought the video game back up again. GAME OVER flashed across the monitor. Something must have killed him when he'd hidden the screen from his mom. "Crap," Josh whispered. He'd been on level twelve, too—the final level. He'd only gotten that far once before.

After his parents called up to say that they were leaving and the front door slammed shut, Josh sighed and clicked back to his history paper. History was the most boring subject in the world. Why did they even make people take it in school? No one *remembered* it. Suddenly, his instant message window started blinking. Josh clicked on it. The program was telling him that someone named GlamSam was trying to IM him. Did he want to accept the message? Josh clicked Accept, although he had no idea who GlamSam was. The message popped on the screen.

    GlamSam: Hey, Josh. U there?

Josh frowned, and replied.

    Trager206: Who is this?
    GlamSam: Sam Jeffries. Remember me from the Halloween store?

Josh nearly tipped over in his leather desk chair. Did he *remember* Samantha Jeffries? That was like asking Kyle if he remembered the first twenty places of pi. Or asking Lori if she remembered which stores at the mall were having sales, and when.

Still, he had to play it very, very cool.

    Trager206: Sure, I remember U. What's up?
    GlamSam: Not much. Just hanging out. What are U up to?

Josh hesitated. He was pretty sure telling her he was doing homework would sound nerdy and lame. Maybe playing video games was lame, too.

Trager206: Just chillin'.

There.

> **GlamSam:** Cool. So I came by to spy on U at football
> practice today. XCept . . . U weren't there. Y?

Josh sat back. Samantha had come to *watch* him
play football? He twirled his red sparkly pen in his fingers, trying to figure a way out of this. The pen had the
words DR. PLATT: BECAUSE GOOD BONES ARE HEALTHY
BONES! printed on it. Dr. Platt was his father's orthope-
dist; his dad went every once in a while
for**REBECCA**an**THATCHER**old basketball knee
injury.

Josh put the pen down and grinned. He had an
idea. *Perfect.*

> **Trager206:** Had an appt. with the orthopedist. My knee's
> messed up—I have to sit out during practice all
> this week.
> **GlamSam:** ☹! I wanted to watch U play!
> **Trager206:** I know. Sucks. But how about I show U some
> of my moves at the Mash?

Josh hit Return. For thirty seconds, Samantha didn't
reply. He wondered if he'd been too forward. If he'd
messed something up. This was Samantha Jeffries.
Every guy wanted her. She probably had sixty guys
calling her to ask her out every day.

Then the IM screen lit up again.

> **GlamSam:** Cool! Meet U there? U like tequila?
> **Trager206:** Absolutely.

Samantha signed off. Josh stared excitedly at the screen. It was happening. Finally, it was really happening for him. Samantha Jeffries. He reached out to his monitor, putting his thumb right over the *xoxoxo* that she'd typed. He caressed the letters as if they were her lips.

But then, a small barb of worry crept into his stomach. His football lie made him a little nervous. He'd bought himself some time, saying he couldn't play football for the whole next week, but what would happen after that? And surely there would be some guys at the Monster Mash who did play on Beachwood's team. What if Samantha asked them about Josh? They'd laugh and tell her that a little runt like him wouldn't even make the JV bench. Could he seriously make this work?

There was another problem, too. Samantha assumed that Josh drank, probably because a lot of the guys on the football team did. Truthfully, he was still an alcohol virgin. Josh wasn't even sure he knew what tequila tasted like or how you were supposed to drink it. Mixed with something? In a shot?

Josh stared at the GAME OVER screen on his video game, feeling nervous. He sort of wished that the Monster Mash chaperones would really crack down this year and do hard-core bag searches at the door and in the parking lot. Maybe his mom would ground him, so he wouldn't have to go at all.

Then he blinked his eyes quickly and shook his head. Was he *nuts*? Of course he had to go. This was the opportunity of a lifetime. But there was no way he could admit to Samantha who he really was—Josh Trager, who was not part of the popular crowd, who loved video games and his skateboard, who knew nothing about drinking, and who had no experience with girls except his brief skinny-dipping encounter with Ashleigh Redmond and the many, many girls he ogled in *Playpen* magazine. If Samantha knew the true Josh, she'd roll her eyes and run into the arms of the many bigger, cooler, more experienced guys who all wanted her, too. So fine—he had to fudge the truth a little. He would deflect the conversation as best as possible from football all night. And he would drink with the best of them, like he'd been doing it for years.

All he needed, then, was a little practice.

Josh padded into the hall and down the stairs. The house was quiet, clean, and smelled like those freaky aromatherapy candles his mom had recently gotten really into. Kyle's bedroom door was shut, and soft music wafted out. Good. Ever studious, Kyle was probably doing his homework. Josh tiptoed into the living room, straight to his parents' tall mahogany liquor cabinet. The bottles gleamed through the glass-paneled doors. Josh tried the knob. His parents had locked it, of course. Not losing hope, Josh walked into the kitchen and flicked on the light. The fluorescent light over the island made him squint. He opened the freezer and peered inside. There was a half bottle of vodka nestled between a box of Popsicles and a deep-dish frozen pizza. Good enough. Josh smiled devilishly, pulled the bottle out, grabbed the hula girl shot glass his dad had gotten on a business trip to Hawaii, and scampered back up to his room.

He put the bottle on his nightstand and poured himself a shot. The vodka was clear, like water. Harmless, right? Taking a deep breath, he shut his eyes and swallowed it. The vodka had no taste, but it burned the whole way down his throat. He stuck his tongue out and tried not to gag. "Be strong," he whispered to himself.

He poured himself two more shots, drank, and waited. And waited. He looked around at the posters on his wall, expecting his vision to get . . . blurry. He recited the alphabet, figuring he'd probably forgotten how . . . only he hadn't. A to Z, no problem—he could even say it backward. The vodka was seriously setting his stomach on fire, but otherwise, he didn't feel much at all.

He fell back on his pillow and put his hands behind his head. Maybe he had some sort of alcohol supertolerance. Maybe drinking was his hidden talent! Josh could just imagine what an asset that would be at the Mash: He and Samantha would belt down tequila at the party. Samantha would become drunker and drunker while Josh would continue to feel perfect. Eventually Samantha would be too drunk to stand, and fall helplessly into Josh's arms. Josh would carry her home, and as he would settle her into bed, Samantha would open her eyes. "Thank you," she'd say to him . . . and then give him the biggest kiss ever. *Swoon*.

"Josh?" Kyle was calling him through the door.

Josh sat up straight. The room lurched. His arms and legs felt like linguine. "What is it?" he called. It came out as one sloppy syllable, which struck him as kind of funny.

"I was just wondering if you wanted to watch a movie or something."

"That's okay," Josh said. He tried to stand, but his balance was off. He tipped over, gripping the bureau for balance, somehow knocking over the wooden baseball bat he'd gotten at a Mariners game when he was ten. It clattered to the floor. "Oops," he muttered.

"Is everything okay?" Kyle sounded concerned.

"Sure," Josh mumbled. He sat back down and tried to breathe in and out. He'd probably just gotten up too fast, that was all. He considered telling Kyle what he'd done, but then he decided against it. Kyle wouldn't get it. He would give Josh that same judging look he'd given him the other day, when Josh said he'd do anything to impress Samantha.

"Okay," Kyle said slowly. "Well, let me know if you change your mind."

Josh listened to Kyle's feet padding away. Once his downstairs bedroom door softly closed, Josh let out a sigh. Okay. Where was he? He eyed the vodka bottle. Time for another shot?

But his head kind of felt like it was going to fall off. Josh hadn't felt this nauseated since he went on the carnival swings when he was five. He'd insisted to his dad he was big enough to ride the adult swings, but when he'd gotten off, he'd walked loopily around in a circle and then puked into a trash can.

Actually he sort of felt like puking now.

Josh stood up, all at once certain he *was* going to puke. He felt a tightness in his throat. His stomach heaved. He burst out his room and ran to the bathroom, bent over halfway. He barely got to the toilet before everything came up.

After it was all over, he wiped his mouth, stood up, and stared at himself in the mirror. His eyes were bloodshot, his face was slick with sweat, and his hair was sticking to his forehead. Okay, *this* was not the look he was going for. If this happened to him at the Mash, he wouldn't even need to tell Samantha the truth about who he really was: she'd take one look at him, scream, and run the other direction.

He washed his mouth out with Listerine, staggered back to his bedroom, and crawled under his covers. He felt too woozy to take the vodka bottle back downstairs, so he kicked it under his bed and promised himself he'd take it down in the morning before his parents were up. He let out a long, uncomfortable sigh. If this was drinking, then he had a lot more practicing to do.

Except . . . hopefully it could wait until tomorrow night.

9. What's in a Name?

At the very same time, Kyle sat in his bathtub in his downstairs bedroom, his knees curled up to his chest, his shoulders resting against the tub's smooth, cold back. He loved his bedroom. Nicole and Stephen had converted it from Stephen's workshop into Kyle's own private sanctuary, and he felt eternally grateful. His drawings hung on the wall. He had his own tub to sleep in and his own computer for Internet surfing. There were stacks and stacks of books in the corners—Kyle had read all of them, of course. Then again, it only took him about twenty minutes to read a whole book.

He had finished his homework and wasn't sure what to do with himself. Stephen and Nicole were out to dinner, Lori was at Hillary's house, and Josh was in his bedroom—probably playing video games. Without distractions, all Kyle could think about was Amanda. It was like he could still smell her honeysuckle perfume and feel her soft hair. But after those wonderful sensations came a horrible one—Amanda had walked away from him today, as if Kyle didn't even exist. As if what they'd just been doing and talking about didn't matter.

Kyle heard the sound of the upstairs toilet flushing over and over again. He contemplated going upstairs and asking Josh again if he was okay but decided against it. Josh hated to be babied any more than he already was. Nicole and Stephen were always keeping their eye on him, certain he was going to get into trouble.

Kyle sighed, got out of the tub, and slipped out the front door. He walked around the house until he came to the tall oak. Kyle climbed the wooden ladder slowly and carefully scooted onto the tree house ledge. He sat for a while, swinging his legs. The night air smelled good, like dewy grass and a wood stove. Next door, Amanda's house was dark and quiet. Her bedroom light wasn't on and her car wasn't in the driveway, meaning she was probably out somewhere. *Out with Charlie, I'll bet,* Kyle thought sadly.

He reached into his pocket and found the little silver cell phone Nicole and Stephen had given him for emergencies. Lori had entered her and Josh's phone numbers, as well as Declan's, Hillary's, and Josh's friend Doug's, in case Kyle couldn't find Lori or Josh. He found Hillary's number and stared at it for a while. Finally, after taking a deep, deep breath, he hit Send. Hillary picked up on the second ring.

"Kyle, what a nice surprise," she cooed. "Does this mean you want to go with me to the Mash after all?"

"I guess," Kyle said in a very small voice.

"And are we craving some Operation Make Her Jealous lessons?"

Kyle blushed in the darkness. He glanced at Amanda's house again, afraid its walls were listening and would tell Amanda what Kyle was planning. "I don't know. Maybe."

"This is perfect," Hillary said excitedly. "You won't regret it, Kyle. I promise. Now, let's see . . ." He heard papers flipping in the background. "How about we have our first session in Mrs. Smythe's study hall tomorrow. Sound good?"

"We're doing this *during* school?" Kyle asked, surprised. He figured Operation Make Her Jealous lessons would have to be super secret—so Amanda wouldn't find out.

"Why not?" Hillary asked. "We'll whisper. Don't stress."

Kyle ended the call, feeling unsettled. He hoped he hadn't made the wrong decision. He hated deceiving Amanda and wished he could just come out and tell her how he felt without all these games. But maybe games were the only way.

Kyle sighed, figuring he should climb down and go back inside. He stared abstractedly over the edge of the tree house, trying to gauge the distance to the ground. The ground *did* seem pretty far away. And yet he'd jumped so easily yesterday. How?

Then again, lots of things that were impossible for most people were easy for Kyle. Like math. Or IQ tests. Or blowing up those balloons today with Amanda. Something inside him told him that his talents—and there were lots of them—should be kept hidden. In school, Kyle knew the answers before the teacher even finished the questions, but when the teacher called on him, he sometimes gave the right answer, but sometimes he forced himself to give the wrong one. He made a mistake or two on quizzes and tests, just because he didn't want to stand out by getting everything correct. In gym class, he had to slow himself down when the boys ran around the track, for fear that if he ran his normal speed, everyone would find it weird. Kids called people who were different all kinds of terrible things every day—*freak, oddball, loser*. It was pretty obvious that being different—even if it was better—wasn't always good.

A light breeze blew against Kyle's face. He watched as the upstairs bathroom light snapped off. What made Kyle so incredible, anyway? Did it have something to do with his blank past? Kyle shut his eyes and tried to remember something. Anything at all. But his memory always started at the same place—waking up at Victor Falls, covered in that pink stuff. Seeing that snake. There was nothing before that except some flashes and shapes. Unconsciously, he slid his hand into his pocket and ran his fingers over the plastic key fob. He'd been carrying it around with him everywhere, and his hands always felt drawn to it.

He opened his eyes and noticed a shadowy movement near the Tragers' garden shed. Kyle frowned, the hair on the back of his neck slowly rising. There was someone down there again.

Kyle's muscles felt electrified. Adrenaline pumped through his veins. His vision seemed to sharpen, as did his reflexes. He slowly crept down the tree house ladder. The person was still there near the shed, but he now seemed to be rummaging around in the bushes, as if he was looking for something. Kyle crept closer and closer. His hand shaped into a fist. He swallowed quietly. Then, suddenly, he stepped on a twig. He froze. The person by the bushes looked up . . . straight at Kyle.

Kyle's mouth fell open. It was Tom Foss, the neighborhood patrolman. Except tonight, Foss was wearing a black hooded sweatshirt and jeans, not his police uniform. He looked unshaven, and his eyes were wild.

Tom Foss stepped back, surprised Kyle was there. He didn't know what to do—he didn't want to make any sudden moves, and he didn't want to scare Kyle. This wasn't the right time to tell him the truth. He needed to get out of here without disrupting anything.

Kyle was staring at him, as if ready to fight. And why shouldn't he be? For all he knew, this was his home. This was his territory to protect. Tom knew he'd taken a risk by coming here and search for the fob . . . but he had no other choice.

"Kyle," Foss said slowly, backing up. "I need your help. I'm looking for something. I'm wondering if you've seen it."

Kyle's mouth dropped open. "How do you know my name?" Yes, Kyle had seen Foss before, but he had definitely never spoken to him.

Foss pushed his hands in his pockets and winced. He assumed Kyle had told him his name the first time they'd met. He hadn't meant to make that mistake. "I . . ."

"How do you know my name?" Kyle repeated. His heart beat faster and faster.

Foss ran his hands through his hair. He began to get frustrated. "I think you have something of mine," he said, his patience growing thin. "I need it back."

"Get off my property," Kyle commanded.

"You don't really live here," Foss said sharply.

Kyle's eyes widened. Who was this guy? How did he know anything about Kyle? "I said, leave."

Foss hunched his shoulders. His eyes flashed. "You have something that belongs to me," he said harshly. "If you don't give it back, you might be in a lot of danger."

"What do you mean?" Kyle demanded.

Then Foss noticed headlights in the driveway. The Tragers were home.

Kyle faced Foss. The car's headlights danced across his shoulders. He didn't know what to do. But then Foss pulled his sweatshirt hood onto his head. He glared at Kyle. "If you tell anyone I was here, you'll be sorry," he growled.

He stepped out of the bushes and ran through the backyard and into the woods. By the time Stephen put the car into park, there was no trace of Foss left.

10. Secrets and Lies

Wednesday morning, Lori sat at the breakfast table, staring at her unfinished trigonometry homework. It might as well have been in Swahili. She wrote down a number, erased, then wrote down another number. But that didn't look right either.

Kyle stopped eating his Cheerios and Sour Patch Kids breakfast—which turned his milk a nasty-looking neon green—and tapped Lori's notebook. "You need to use the Pythagorean theorem," he said. He took Lori's pencil and wrote down some numbers. "So X equals six."

Lori stared at the page. "Okay," she murmured. She didn't really understand what Kyle just said, but she was certain Kyle was right. Kyle was *always* right when it came to math. She put down her pencil and looked at Kyle. "Hillary told me about your Mash costumes yesterday. They sound fun."

Kyle sipped his orange juice. "Costumes?"

Lori frowned. "You're going as Cinderella and Prince Charming, right? Hillary said she already got her dress, and she's going to pick up your suit tomorrow."

"This is the first I've heard of it," Kyle said slowly.

Lori ran her finger around the top of her striped coffee mug. Leave it to Hillary to plan their Mash costumes and not even tell Kyle about it.

"Are you okay?" she asked. Kyle seemed jumpy and

distracted. He kept scooping up a spoonful of cereal and letting it all fall back into his bowl without eating any of it.

"I'm fine," Kyle said uncomfortably. Although he really wasn't. Because of Hillary, because of Amanda, because of Tom Foss's threats . . . Lori could take her pick. Everything was setting him off today.

"If you don't want to take Hillary to the**THE**Mash, don't," Lori said. She still didn't know what to think about Hillary taking Kyle. There was something so predatory about Hillary's crush on him. Lori worried that by the time the Mash was over, Hillary would have gotten Kyle drunk, deflowered him, and he'd return home with Hillary's**PHOTO**name tattooed on his head. Part of her wanted Kyle to back out of the date with Hillary and realize he could pursue Amanda another way. Then again, it was Kyle's life. If this was what he wanted to do, Lori couldn't exactly stop him.

"No, I'll go with her," Kyle said. "It's fine."

"What's fine?" Lori's mother swept into the room. She was wearing a white pinstriped blazer over a burnt orange dress, and was**HOLDS**carrying her shoes, a large file folder, and her enormous navy-blue leather purse under her arms. She dumped the file on the island, poured some coffee into her chrome travel mug, and groaned when her cell phone**THE**started to ring. Her mother was frantic every morning and always seemed to be running late.

"Nothing," Kyle and Lori said at the same time.

Mrs. Trager stopped her whirlwind activity and raised an eyebrow at both of them. She had that you-two-can't-fool-me look.

Josh slumped into the kitchen. He had**KEY**his hood pulled tight around his head and his arms crossed over his chest. There were dark circles around his eyes, and his skin had a greenish tint to it. "Morning," he mumbled.

"Are you all right?" Mrs. Trager asked, alarmed. "You look sick."

"I'm fine," Josh answered. "I just didn't sleep well last night or something."

Lori looked at her brother suspiciously. *Yeah, right.* Josh had snored loudly the whole night. His bedroom was next to hers, and the noise seeped through the walls. She'd had to sleep with a pillow over her head.

"Can I get you something to eat?" Mrs. Trager asked, fastening her dangling, fan-shaped earrings. "Granola bar?"

Josh's mouth wobbled. His skin turned even greener. "That's okay," he croaked. "I'll just have some toast."

Lori stared at him as he sat down. Something was going on here. Last night, when she'd come home from Hillary's, Josh's bedroom light had been off. Usually Josh pushed his 11 P.M. bedtime to the last possible minute. And she *swore* the upstairs bathroom smelled like puke.

She slowly smiled. Her parents *were* out last night . . .

Josh put his head down on the table. Lori cleared her throat. "So. Still meeting Sam Jeffries at the Mash?"

"Uh-huh," Josh said from between his hands.

"You know she's crazy, right?" Lori asked. "I hear she, like, yells at guys if they don't do what she wants."

"She's not a yeller," Josh scoffed, raising his head. "That's totally a lie."

"She's a big drinker, too, isn't she?" Lori twirled her pencil around in her fingers. Josh gave her a dirty look.

"Who's this?" their mom asked, taking a sip of her coffee. "Is that the girl you're taking to the dance? Does she drink, Josh?"

"No, Mom." Josh groaned. "Lori's lying."

Mrs. Trager stared uneasily at all of them, then shook her head and vanished into the laundry room. When she was gone, Lori leaned forward and gave Josh a fake-sympathetic look. "Hangovers suck, don't they?"

Josh glowered at her. How did Lori guess about his little vodka experiment last night? He'd been super-anal about hiding everything, cleaning up all the little vomit stains in the bathroom with a *toothbrush* before he passed out last night. "I'm not hungover," he mumbled.

"Josh, you're a classic case. Don't even try to fool me. You want some advice? Get an Egg McMuffin on the way to school. Or something greasy like that. The fat will absorb all the booze."

"What's a hangover?" Kyle asked.

"Very funny," Josh whispered to Lori, ignoring Kyle. "You're just jealous because I have a date to the Mash and you don't."

"Shut *up*." Lori's face burned. She was about to retort—something along the lines of *Everyone knows Samantha Jeffries is a slutty, psycho moron*—but her cell phone interrupted her. Hillary's name and photo appeared in the preview window. She sighed.

"What's up?" Lori asked, flipping her phone open.

"I wanted to call you right away," Hillary said. By the whooshing sound, Lori could tell Hillary was in her car. "Have you seen Lila's blog this morning?"

Lori shrugged. "Why would I read Lila's blog?" Lila Thompson was a freshman who kept a blog of school gossip. Other freshmen were the only ones who read it.

"You should check it out," Hillary said. "Lila lists all the people who have dates to the Monster Mash. And you know who's on that list? Declan."

"What?" Lori shrieked, standing up so abruptly that her knees bumped against the bottom of the table. Both Kyle and Josh looked at her. There was a startled look on Kyle's face and a nauseated one on Josh's, like they were all in a canoe and had just accidentally paddled into some rapids. Josh clutched his stomach and bolted down the hall for the bathroom.

"Who is it? Did the blog say?" Lori continued, lowering her voice. She sat back down with as much composure as she could muster.

"It didn't," Hillary answered. "And I don't know. It might be a lie, Lor."

Lori's head spun. Without even realizing, she'd drained the rest of her coffee and dribbled a little bit down the front of her blouse. If Lila's blog was true, it meant Declan had lied to her yesterday in gym when he'd said he was going alone. Why would he do that? To spare her feelings? What, did Declan think she *cared* or something?

Lori racked her brain to figure out who Declan's date might be. There was a cheerleader she'd seen him talking to in the hallways. Or there was Jessica, the slutty sophomore Declan had been kissing at his party this summer. Lori gritted her teeth. She just *bet* it was Jessica—rumor had it she'd made out with a guy in the principal's office.

When she looked up, she noticed that Kyle was reading the back of the Cheerios box. Only, there was nothing *on* the back of the Cheerios box except a big picture of a bowl of cereal, a glass of orange juice, and some toast. It was obvious he was listening to her conversation but pretending that he wasn't.

Lori got up from her seat, messily stuffed her math homework into her olive-green canvas tote, and drifted into the hall. "It doesn't matter," she said into her phone. "Declan can take whomever he wants. I don't care. He's a jerk and he—he has death breath. Everyone knows it, too." It was a lie, but she had to think of something bad about Declan. She shut her phone with a flourish and slumped against the wall.

A few seconds of silence passed. Kyle dropped his spoon in his bowl and walked into the hall. Lori was standing next to the wall of family photos, her chin tucked against her chest.

"What's the matter?" Kyle asked in a low voice.

"Nothing," Lori snapped, not meeting Kyle's eye. Her cheeks were starting to get hot. Her eyes began to sting. She turned away, slung her bag over her shoulder, and dashed upstairs to her room. She had to get out of there before she lost it.

Kyle didn't know what else to do but to return to the breakfast table. He ate another soggy bite of Cheerios and Sour Patch Kids after he heard Lori's bedroom door slam. Nicole reappeared from the laundry room and looked confusedly at the table. "Where did everyone go?"

Kyle shrugged, not sure how much he should say.

Nicole walked around the side of the island and sat down in Lori's vacated place. She studied Lori's half-uneaten doughnut, then took a bite out of it. "So how are you doing, Kyle?"

Kyle shrugged. "All right, I guess."

"Lori told me you're going to the Monster Mash

with her friend Hillary. And you're going as Prince Charming and Cinderella."

Kyle smirked. It was amazing that even Nicole knew about the costumes before he did. "I guess so," he said, a little somberly.

Nicole gave him a surprised look. "I thought you might be little more into it than that. Prince Charming isn't your cup of tea, huh?"

Kyle shrugged. "Prince Charming is fine," he said. "I just . . . I've been thinking about Halloween a lot lately," he finally said. "I still don't get the point of it. I mean, I understand it's the one day where you dress up and get to be someone else, but I still don't really get *why*."

"For fun," Nicole said, turning her palms up.

"It just seems like lying," Kyle answered. "Dressing up as someone else seems like you're hiding stuff."

Nicole leaned forward on her elbows. "That's an awfully serious interpretation of Halloween." She paused for a moment, examining Kyle carefully. "You know what I think? This isn't about Halloween at all. There's something else bothering you."

Kyle gazed into the back of his cereal spoon. He could see a warped version of his face—his nose and lips were huge, his eyes small, the background curved and exaggerated. He thought about telling Nicole about his feelings for Amanda, but she would probably tell Kyle that he should be respectful of Amanda's relationship with Charlie and back off. And Nicole certainly wouldn't approve of Operation Make Her Jealous.

But far worse than his Amanda worries was what happened with Foss last night. Kyle shut his eyes. Every time he thought of Foss, a piercing, uneasy ache zigzagged through his stomach. How did Foss know his name? Was Foss from his past? Kyle thought about what Foss said last night: *You have something of mine. If you keep it, you're putting yourself in danger.* Did Foss mean the key fob? Why would a silly key fob be so important—or dangerous? What did it access? And then he had told Kyle not to tell the Tragers . . . or else. Kyle didn't know what to do. If Kyle told Nicole and Stephen, what if something happened to him . . . or them?

Kyle peeked at Nicole. She was staring at him, waiting for his answer. He knew he should have told them about Foss last night, as soon as it happened. If he told Nicole now, she might wonder if Kyle was hiding something, something that had held him back from telling her earlier. Lying to her made him feel awful, like he was unworthy of her kindness and gratitude. Like he was repaying all their kindness with a secret that could potentially cause them harm.

"Have you ever kept a secret about something because you thought it was the right thing to do, even if it meant lying?" Kyle blurted out.

Nicole narrowed her eyes, trying to interpret Kyle's question. "Are you keeping a secret for Lori or Josh?" she asked slowly, looking suspicious. "Did they ask you to do something like that for them again?" Kyle had been caught up in Lori and Josh's schemes before, and Nicole was always trying to keep him out of trouble.

Kyle shrugged, not quite able to look at her. "This has nothing to do with Lori or Josh. It's just a—a hypothetical question." He thought for a moment. He wanted to explain the Foss thing to her but couldn't bring himself to do it. "There was a scenario like it in one of Josh's video games—someone has to keep a secret about something, even though he has to lie to the others to keep them safe."

Nicole sighed, crossing her arms over her chest. "Josh plays too many video games. Don't let him suck you in." She patted his arm. "But back to your issues with Halloween—are you sure they don't have to do with your amnesia and your missing identity? Perhaps *you* feel like you're in costume, because you can't remember who you are?" She paused but didn't wait for Kyle to answer. "You shouldn't stress over that, Kyle. I know it's not fair, and it's natural to be frustrated. Why did *you* get stuck with amnesia? What did *you* do to deserve it? Remember: you didn't do anything to deserve it. And it's not fair. And you have every right to be angry. But you can't give up hope—your memory *will* come back, Kyle. I'm here to help you through that. However long it takes. Okay?"

"Okay," Kyle mumbled, staring at his shoes.

"Good." Nicole stood up and gave Kyle a hug. "We'd better get going. Otherwise, we're going to be hideously late."

Kyle silently walked back to his bedroom to get his backpack. He felt guilty—Nicole had been so nice and comforting, unaware that Kyle was hiding a huge lie.

As he slid his backpack straps over his shoulders, something on his desk caught his eye. He had forgotten about the drawing he'd completed last night, long after everyone else had gone to sleep. He'd scribbled it so quickly and frantically, just getting it down on the page so he could get it out of his head. He hadn't even cleaned up his chalks afterward—they still lay scattered and cracked around the paper.

Kyle shakily lifted the drawing up to the light. Tom Foss stared back at him, crouched down near the Tragers' shed. Kyle had managed to capture a desperate glimmer in Foss's eyes. The man's mouth hung open, revealing his crooked bottom teeth. The picture was so realistic, Kyle almost expected the Foss on the paper to call out Kyle's name and warn Kyle not to utter a word of this to anyone.

All of a sudden, Kyle felt that itchy feeling at the back of his neck again. He looked around his bedroom. Dust particles lit up by the morning sun danced through the air. His bathtub bed glimmered. His comforter lay in a clump near one of the tub's ends. His laptop whirred silently on his desk. A bird landed on a tree branch outside his window. Kyle was alone. And yet . . . it really felt like he wasn't.

"Kyle?" Nicole called from the foyer. "Want me to give you a ride? We're leaving now!"

"Okay," Kyle said back. He looked at the drawing once more. Then, with a few swift movements, he tore it into tiny pieces and threw it into the trash.

11. See What Develops

The third period bell rang, and Kyle slid into his study hall seat. He watched as Hillary sauntered down the aisle and fell into the chair behind him. The class was quiet for a few minutes, but once Mrs. Smythe, the study hall teacher, buried her nose in her latest romance novel—a huge book with a busty, half-naked woman on its purple cover—Kyle felt Hillary's finger tap his shoulder.

"You ready?" she whispered.

"I guess," Kyle answered, not feeling ready at all.

"We can sit at the table in the back." Hillary stood and motioned for Kyle to follow. The study hall took place in one of the photography studios. It always smelled strongly of chemicals, and students constantly filtered in and out to work in the dark room. All of the tables and shelves were full of photo books; extra bottles of developing and fixing chemicals; negatives; film canisters; and rejected, badly developed photos. The door that led to a separate, smaller room that held the equipment for digital photography was always locked. Off to the right of the room was a revolving door that led to the darkroom itself, which was big; secluded; filled with high-tech enlargers; and lit by tiny, dim red lightbulbs. There was a big sign on the darkroom door that said DARKROOM FOR PHOTO-DEVELOPING PURPOSES ONLY! VIOLATORS WILL GET DETENTION! The photo teacher had to put it up because a lot of couples liked to duck into the darkroom to make out.

"Okay." Hillary pushed a few random handouts, film canisters, and photo boxes aside, plopped a blue binder on the table, and sat down. She rolled up the sleeves of her silk blouse and crossed her long, mostly bare legs. "I'm so excited you decided to do this, Kyle," she gushed, snapping her gum. "It's totally going to work. I promise you."

Kyle tried to smile.

"Operation Make Her Jealous." Hillary opened the binder and pointed to the cover page, which said the same thing.

"You're really organized," Kyle said, impressed. "Have you done this before?"

"Not exactly." Hillary leaned forward. "Although I *should*. I should write all this down in a book. I'd probably get tons of money for it."

She flipped to the next page. There were only two words on it: *Hot Commodity*. Hillary folded her hands professionally. "Okay. You want Amanda, right?" Kyle nodded. "The trouble is, she's more complicated than other girls. She's so . . . good . . . meaning it might be a little tougher to drag her away from Charlie. I'm sure she has some crazy notion in her head that they're in love and that she shouldn't even *think* about other guys as long as she's with him. And I'm sure she's *never* broken up with a guy before. She's totally not the type."

"How do you know all this?" Kyle asked, amazed.

"Because I'm the expert," Hillary said, flirtatiously tapping Kyle on the arm. "Anyway. Don't worry. *Every* girl can be cracked, even Amanda. All we need to do is make Amanda think that you, Kyle, are in demand. The hottest boy in school that every girl at Beachwood wants to date."

Kyle scratched his head. He didn't *feel* like the hottest

boy in Beachwood that every girl wanted to date. "How do I do that?"

"We've got the first part covered," Hillary said. She started absentmindedly flipping through a stack of cast-off black-and-white photos next to the chemicals. Most of them hadn't been developed properly and were either dark and shadowy or white and washed-out. "These all suck," she murmured, tossing the images aside.

Then she turned back to Kyle. "You and I are going to the Monster Mash together," she stated, "but I'm not sure that's effective enough. We need something else to really drive the point home. How about we start a rumor saying that ten other girls also asked you to the Mash? But, naturally you had to decline because you're taking me."

Kyle frowned. "But that's not true."

Hillary widened her blue eyes. "We have to make it look like you're in demand, Kyle. This is how you do it." She snapped her fingers. "And I just thought of the most brilliant thing to go with that rumor. A lot of girls wanted to go with you because you are this *amazing* kisser. Like, you know lots of superromantic moves that most guys at Beachwood just ignore." A conniving grin slithered onto her face. "That is *so* perfect. Amanda seems like just the type who would go for all that sappy romantic stuff."

Kyle ran his hands through his hair and stared absently at some of the photos on the wall. They were all of landscapes, people's feet, or the Seattle skyline. "But . . . I don't know if I'm an amazing kisser. And I don't know any superromantic moves."

Hillary's eyes lit up. "Want me to teach you some?" She glanced over at the darkroom's door.

Kyle shook his head nervously. He wasn't even entirely sure what kissing was. You press your lips together . . . and then what? Does something else happen? Was it easy to tell if you had no experience? He ran his tongue over his teeth. Maybe Lori was right. Maybe Operation Make Her Jealous was a horrible, horrible idea.

Hillary shrugged it off. "It doesn't matter that you have no experience with girls. After we plant the rumor, it'll basically be fact. And once Amanda hears it, the gears will start turning in her head, and she'll realize that maybe you're a better catch than Charlie." Hillary sighed dramatically. "You really should be thanking me, Kyle. After all this, so many girls will want to date you, it won't even matter if Amanda is interested. Most guys would kill for my help with this. I should be charging you a fee or something."

Kyle took the stack of badly processed photos from Hillary and started to flip through them nervously, just so he had something to do with his hands. "So how are you going to start this rumor?" he asked.

Hillary giggled. "Starting the rumor is easy. All I have to do is leak it to Lila Thompson. She adores gossip—she'll have it up on her blog by this afternoon."

"And will Amanda read Lila's blog?"

"Even if she doesn't, she'll hear about it. *Everybody* hears about the gossip on Lila's blog." Hillary laid her hands flat on the table. "So basically the only thing *you* have to do is not deny the whole thing. You don't have to talk yourself up or anything, just don't admit that any of it isn't true. Can you do that?"

Kyle swallowed hard. He had no idea. What if Amanda asked Kyle about the rumors directly? What would he say? And surely Amanda knew him better than that—didn't she? Amanda would never believe that Kyle had kissed a girl—let alone a bunch of them. He felt like his inexperience was written all over him in thick marker.

"I'm also counting on you to tell Amanda that you have a big date to the Mash," Hillary instructed. "Pretend like you're really excited about taking me. Use these exact words: you have a *hot date,* and it's going to be a *major hookup fest.*"

Kyle committed the words to memory.

"There's one more thing," Hillary said. She flipped through her binder again. There was only one word in big, bold letters in the center of the next page: *PDA.* She pointed to it. "I think we will need a lot of this at the Mash."

Kyle was afraid to ask, but he had to. "PDA?"

"Public displays of affection," Hillary whispered, tapping her finger forcefully on the table to punctuate each word. She crossed her arms and sat back, waiting for Kyle's reaction.

"You and . . . me?" Kyle asked.

"Duh!" Hillary looked at him. "If Amanda sees you making out with me, it will drive her crazy. I'm sure of it. She'll begin to wonder what it would be like to go out with you. She'll see us slow-dancing across the room, gazing into each other's eyes as if we're totally in love, and just *seethe* with jealousy." Hillary broke into a wide, excited grin. "Charlie will be history."

Kyle's head spun. He didn't want anyone seething, especially not Amanda. And he wasn't sure if he could make out with Hillary. Frankly, the idea of kissing Hillary made him a little . . . woozy. "I'm not an actor," Kyle whispered. "I don't know if I can do this."

"Don't worry." Hillary put her hand on Kyle's arm.

As she leaned in close, Kyle caught a whiff of her heady, spicy perfume and sharp spearmint gum. "I'll guide you through the whole thing. And no strings attached between you and me. I promise." She shut the binder. "I'll get started on planting that rumor ASAP. You talk up your hot date and our major hookup fest to Amanda. Okay?"

Kyle paused. He felt like as soon as he said yes, this wouldn't be in his hands anymore. The plan would be in motion. Hillary would start the rumor, Amanda would hear about it, and . . . and then what?

He stared at the photographs on the table. There were six or seven at the bottom of the stack that looked as if they were all the same image—the photographer must have been experimenting with developing techniques. There were a few that were blurry, two that were overexposed, and one that was too dark. But the last picture in the pile was sharp. It was of the Beachwood High courtyard during lunch. A group of girls sat on a picnic table, their heads thrown back in laughter. A boy was playing with his PSP. Two other girls leaned over their cell phones, and some boys were playing ultimate Frisbee on the lawn.

And then, Kyle noticed it: Amanda and Charlie were at the very corner of the photo, sitting alone on a bench. They were looking in opposite directions, like they lived on completely different planets.

Hillary leaned over and looked at the photo, too. "Whoa," she gasped, noticing Charlie and Amanda. "It's totally a sign."

Kyle examined Amanda's distracted expression. It was amazing that Amanda had been there all along, hiding underneath the previous photos' overexposed whiteness, underexposed darkness, and incorrectly processed streakiness. He wondered if there were things Amanda was concealing about herself, too—maybe even things about her relationship with Charlie. Was she really happy? Was Charlie right for her? With the right encouragement, perhaps those answers could be revealed, the same way developing chemicals draw an image out of a photo negative.

Maybe it was a sign. Maybe Amanda had hidden in this photo, waiting and waiting for Kyle to find her.

"So are you in?" Hillary asked again.

"I'm in," Kyle said quietly, pushing the photo back into the stack. He felt a little like he'd taken a huge leap—and not from somewhere manageable like the top of a tree but from the top of the Seattle Space Needle. Or, for that matter, from a space shuttle orbiting Earth.

Hillary clapped her hands. "I'll get started right now."

12. Communication Breakdown

Lori breathed a sigh of relief when the last bell of the Wednesday school day rang. She got up from her desk in history class and shot out into the busy hallway. Her brain felt foggy. She'd floated through school today in a murky haze, not really paying attention to anything that went on around her. She could only think of one thing—*Declan lied to me. He lied, he lied, he lied.*

She had been racking her brain, trying to figure out who Declan was taking to the Mash instead of her. She'd scoped out girls in class and had a new theory each period. Was it Brianna Peters, the shy girl in Jewelry II who allegedly smoked lots of pot? Or what about Denise Jablonski, the captain of the girls' cross-country team? Lori had kept her ears open all day for rumors of who Declan's date might be, except she hadn't heard a thing.

"Hey, Lori." A freshman girl Callie Wright grabbed her arm. "Have you heard the rumors?"

Lori stopped, her stomach sinking. "What—about Declan?"

"I haven't heard anything about Declan." Callie looked a little thrown off track. She pushed a lock of curly brown hair behind her ear. "Actually, it's about that dude who lives in your house. Kyle."

Lori made a face. "Kyle?"

Callie clutched her hands lustfully. She leaned in closer. "Is it true tons of girls come over to your house to see him?"

"And that, before this, he used to be**DON'T**an Abercrombie model?" Another freshman girl, Fern Jacobs, came up behind them. Fern liked to wear her Beachwood High cheerleading uniform even on the days the team wasn't required to. Sometimes she even carried around her pom-poms.

Lori stared at both them blankly. It took her a moment to catch on—of *course*. Hillary. Operation Make Her Jealous or whatever she was calling it. Lori ran her hands through her hair. "Uh . . ."

Callie slammed her locker door**GIVE**shut and pushed her bleached-calfskin purse higher on her shoulder. "God, who knew? He seems so quiet. But he's also really cute."

"Yeah, but he's like under-the-radar cute," Fern pointed out. "Like a brand of makeup that doesn't advertise on**UP**TV or in magazines—you just have to *know* about it. But once you buy it, you never go back to your old stuff. You're like, 'Where has this stuff been all my life?'"

"Totally," Callie agreed. "I was like that with that new line they have at the makeup**THE**store at the mall."

Lori wanted to giggle. She couldn't believe they were comparing Kyle to *makeup*.

"Anyway, he's a major hottie," Fern said. "You're so lucky you see him all the time."

Lori turned away, not able to look the girls in the eye. She felt a little jealous. Hillary had really outdone herself this time—she'd stoked the gossip fire and now it was a four-alarm inferno. Her idiotic make-her-jealous plan would**RING**probably work.

Lori saw a familiar spiky head appear down the hall and sucked in her stomach. *Declan.* He was coming this way. "I have to go," she blurted to the girls, turning and rushing in the opposite direction. There was no way she wanted to see him.

There was a bottleneck of people at the front door. Lori smushed up against two younger boys in front of her, wanting to elbow her way past them and get out the door before Declan got too close. "Come *onnnn*," she said with clenched teeth, standing on tiptoes to see what the holdup was. Finally the throng started moving again. Lori ducked to the right, trying to get around a couple of slow-moving freshmen wearing furry panda backpacks, when suddenly she collided with someone. She looked up, and her stomach tightened.

"Lori, hey." Declan grinned. "I've been looking for you."

Lori felt a mix of rage and shame. Why was he looking for her—so he could lie some more? She turned back around and scrambled down the front steps as fast as she could. A bunch of students was loitering around the courtyard's picnic tables and weeping willow trees, enjoying their first few minutes of after-school freedom. It was one of those perfect fall afternoons where there were colorful little leaf piles in the yard and the air smelled crisp and sweet.

"Lori," Declan called. He followed her. He caught her arm. "Whoa. Hey. Hello? What's the matter?"

Lori reluctantly stopped. She scowled up at him. "What do you want?"

Declan raised his palms into the air, making his Livestrong bracelet slide down his wrist. "I want . . . I don't know. I'm just trying to be friendly. Why are you giving me such attitude? What did I do?"

Lori's mouth fell open. "What did you *do*? You really don't know?"

Declan blinked. "No."

"Wow." Lori shook her head, flabbergasted. "If you don't know, then I'm not going to bother to tell you."

She tried to get away, but Declan blocked her path again. "Is this about us sleeping together at Preston's party?" he asked. "Because, I mean, I thought we talked about that."

It felt like the courtyard had suddenly gotten very quiet, and that Declan had shouted it through a megaphone. Lori was sure a whole bunch of heads had turned in their direction. The words *sleeping together* seemed to echo off the benches, the sidewalks, and the flagpole; and she was almost positive she heard someone gasp.

Lori blinked furiously at Declan. "Thanks for *telling everyone*."

Declan looked helpless. "Lori, I—"

"Excuse me," she interrupted, pushing past him. All she wanted to do right now was lie down. In a grave.

"Lori!" Declan cried after her.

But Lori didn't stop. She stumbled blindly across the courtyard, not even caring that she was stamping down the flower beds and scaring away the squirrels that always nestled by the big oak tree. Then a familiar face swam into view. Kyle sat alone on top of a picnic table. He was staring straight at Lori, clearly having seen and heard the whole thing.

Lori walked up to him and just stood there, her arms crossed tightly over her chest. Her whole body felt like it was blushing, and she was so angry her teeth chattered and her limbs shook. "Is Declan still standing there?" she asked Kyle.

Kyle looked around Lori. "Yes." Declan stared at both of them, his hands on his hips and a baffled, annoyed expression on his face.

Lori groaned. She shut her eyes. "And did you hear what Declan just said?"

Kyle looked back and forth. "Yes."

Lori let out a small whimper. "Which means the rest of the courtyard did, too."

"He looks really confused," Kyle pointed out, "and hurt."

"Why should I care?" Lori exploded, enraged. "He hurt me! How would you like it if someone blurted out a huge secret about *you* right in front of tons and tons of people?"

"I don't know if anyone even understood what he meant," Kyle reasoned. "I mean, so what? You were sleeping together. Why does it matter? It's just sleep."

Lori stared at him. Suddenly she realized—Captain Clueless Kyle had no idea what sleeping together *meant*. "Whatever," she said. A few feet away, a girl's cell phone started ringing, playing a cheerful tune. The girl squealed with laughter. Lori wanted to walk over and wring her neck for being so happy. "I don't want to be alive right now," she muttered. "I feel like everyone's staring at me, thinking, *Oh, poor Lori. She slept with him at Preston's party and now Declan's not even taking her to the Mash!*"

"You still like him, don't you," Kyle said slowly.

Lori smiled bitterly. "Aren't you perceptive?" Her voice dripped sarcasm. She covered her face with her hands again. "Who cares if I like him? He doesn't like me back. Maybe I can transfer schools." She looked up and shook her head. "There's absolutely no way I'm going to the Monster Mash, now."

"Why not?" Kyle asked.

"Didn't I just explain this?" Lori's eyes widened. "It's too embarrassing. I don't want to see him with another girl. If I go, Declan will think that I'm . . . stalking him. That I like him."

"But you *do* like him," Kyle repeated. "Why can't you just tell him that?"

Lori smacked the side of her head. She was tempted to smack Kyle's, too. "What planet are you from? That is just about the stupidest advice ever."

Kyle picked at a loose piece of wood on the picnic table bench. "But if you were just honest with him, maybe you'd find out he likes you, too."

Lori glared at Kyle. "Listen to you, giving me a lecture on honesty! I heard a rumor about you just now, Kyle. Apparently all the girls are all over you. Now who do you think started something like that?"

Kyle felt the blood drain from his face. He was surprised that Operation Make Her Jealous had gotten off the ground so fast.

"It's not like you're telling the truth either." Lori slumped against the picnic table, pressing her sneaker into a divot of grass. "So keep your advice to yourself."

"Okay," Kyle said quietly. "I'm sorry."

"Whatever." Lori bit her lip and took a deep breath. It was hard to quell the sobs welling up inside her.

"He's gone now," Kyle said, watching as Declan shrugged, then started loping dejectedly toward the parking lot.

"Good." Lori sat down on the picnic table bench and stared at the ground. "And don't you *dare* tell anyone what I just said. As far as we're concerned, we never had this conversation."

"Fine," Kyle said quickly.

A few seconds passed. Some school buses rolled away from the curb, spitting black clouds of exhaust. A group of sophomores bounded down the front stairs, singing at the top of their lungs. Lori bent over her legs and let the tears roll silently down her cheeks and into her mouth. They tasted salty.

There were so many things that made her angry right now. Declan was taking someone else, he had just embarrassed her, and now she couldn't go to the dance. Worse, *Kyle* had witnessed her breakdown. Lori liked to keep her emotions under wraps as much as she could, but this Declan thing was turning her into a crazy person. She wanted to dive into Puget Sound and sink to the bottom.

Lori stared at Kyle's sneakers through the gaps in her fingers. He sat silently next to her. They both stayed like that for a long time, each lost in thought. They both felt tormented about their private, innermost feelings becoming public. Neither had any idea how they were going to deal.

13. Ghosts
in the Graveyard

The next day, Kyle and Amanda stood in the Beachwood Rec Center. They stared at their finished mural, which was still wet. They'd finished painting the entire grave scene, using some real names from tombstones from the graveyard across the street. They had also painted a gray wolf howling at the moon and a bunch of vaporous ghosts, rising eerily out of the ground and floating into the sky. Amanda had done all the preliminary painting, and Kyle had gone over it all in the unique, stippled style he used when drawing. It made the mural look practically like a photograph.

"It looks amazing," Kyle said, dropping his used paintbrush on a pile of newspapers.

"Doesn't it?" Amanda seconded. She put her hands on her hips. "We did a great job."

As Kyle glanced at Amanda, his mind swirled. Hillary's rumors were out there. How far had they gotten? Had Amanda heard about them? Would they impress her, or would she just think they were weird?

"What'cha thinking about?" Amanda asked.

Kyle jumped. "The—the mural," he stammered.

Amanda put her hands in her pockets. "Me, too. I can't wait for everyone to see it." She glanced at Kyle. "I really owe all this to you, Kyle. I couldn't have done any of this without your help."

"It was fun," Kyle said quietly.

They locked eyes for a moment. Kyle felt like he might explode. He turned and stared again at the mural. "So do you believe in ghosts?" he asked, studying the ones they'd just painted on the wall.

Amanda paused, thinking. "I believe in nice ghosts. Ones that don't want to hurt you. They come for friendly reasons and help you through things."

She sat down on the floor and started organizing the cans of paint. Kyle noticed she looked contemplative, like she wanted to say more but wasn't sure if she should. He sat down next to her. "Did you have a ghost who helped you through something?"

"I don't know," Amanda said quietly. Sunlight from the window danced across her face, making her look angelic. "When my dad died, I felt like there was . . . this spirit with me. It's hard to explain."

"Do you think it was your dad?" Kyle asked.

"Not exactly." Amanda shook her head. "This is probably crazy, but the ghost seemed sort of grandmotherly. The kind of lady who bakes pies and knits. I felt like she was just . . . watching me. Making sure I got up in the morning and went to school. Staying by my side as I slept. I felt safe. I even had a name for her."

"What?" Kyle asked.

Amanda shook her head, biting her lip. "It's silly."

"Tell me."

She giggled. "Gertrude. I have no idea why." She waved her hand. "I'm embarrassed."

"Don't be," Kyle said softly. "That sounds nice. Do you think Gertrude is still here?"

Amanda shook her head. "After a while, she just . . . stopped coming." She glanced at him quickly, then looked away. "I've never told anyone about this except you."

Kyle's heart started beating faster. "Why not?"

Amanda shrugged. "I'd never tell my mom. She'd just say I was crazy. She might even get angry. And Charlie . . ." She looked uncomfortable. "I don't know. Charlie wouldn't be interested, either."

Kyle picked at the label on one of the paint cans, not wanting to seem too eager. "He *should* be interested. He's your boyfriend."

"Yeah, well . . ." Amanda clucked her tongue. "We don't tell each other everything."

Kyle shivered. He wondered what Amanda meant by that.

Amanda started to clean up the painting supplies, rolling all the brushes in the newspaper and making sure all the paint can lids were on tight. "Anyway, I read about this way to conjure up spirits, and I always wanted to try. The only problem is you need two people."

"I'll do it with you," Kyle said.

Amanda peeked at him, then looked away fast. "That's okay, Kyle. You don't have to."

"No, really," Kyle said. "I'd be happy to." He liked the idea of ghosts—spirits and phantoms most of the world couldn't see, hiding out on Earth. Maybe everyone had a personal ghost . . . maybe even Kyle. Perhaps his ghost could fill him in on who he was, where he had been all these years. Why Foss knew his name.

Amanda stacked the paint cans near the wall and wiped her hands on a paper towel. "It doesn't matter anyway. The only day the spell can work is Halloween. Not that it's going to work at all, of course."

"So why don't we do it on Halloween?" Kyle goaded.

Amanda stared at him. "The Mash is Halloween. Remember?"

"So? Couldn't we do it afterward?"

Amanda paused. She gave Kyle an uncomfortable smile. "I'm supposed to go to a party afterward. With Charlie."

"Do you have to?" Kyle blurted out.

"Well, yeah. He's my boyfriend. And my date to the Mash."

"Right." Kyle turned away, clenching his stomach with embarrassment. "I didn't mean . . ." He stared at the floor.

Amanda's posture instantly became stiff and formal. All the energy that had been zapping between them just seconds ago had vanished. Suddenly Kyle remembered. Operation Make Her Jealous! He hadn't done a single thing Hillary had advised.

"Actually I have a date, too," he said in a loud, false voice, "to the Mash."

Amanda looked surprised. "You do?"

"Yep," Kyle said, trying to remember exactly what Hillary told him to say. "A hot date. *Amazingly* hot." The words felt positively idiotic coming out of his mouth.

Amanda burst out laughing. "You just sounded like you channeled a girl."

Kyle shrugged. "It's going to be a huge hookup fest."

Amanda giggled again, but when she met Kyle's eyes, she stopped. "You're serious, aren't you?" Kyle nodded. He watched as Amanda's expression went from surprise to disappointment to something that resembled happiness . . . although not quite.

"Well, that's great, Kyle," she said in a soft voice. "I'm really happy for you. Who is it?"

Kyle was about to answer when there was a thud from the haunted house. All the boys tumbled out, shoving one another and laughing. Amanda's gaze shifted off Kyle and to Charlie, who was among the pack. "Hey!" she cried, waving at Charlie with her whole arm. "Over here!"

No, Kyle thought. *Please not now.* His heart plummeted to his shoes.

But Charlie was already running over. "What's up?"

"Not much," Amanda answered. "Just finishing up. All I have to do is clean these brushes and I'll be done."

"Cool, cool. Me, too. We can go home together." Charlie reached in his jeans pocket for his car keys. "So the haunted house is going to be sick this year," he boasted. "It is going to be scare central. Even the guys are going to be squealing like little girls."

"That's great," Amanda cooed, touching his nose. "I'm sure everyone's going to love it."

"Everyone's going to love our mural, too," Kyle said, pointing feebly at the wall. Charlie hadn't even bothered to look at their decorations, even though they'd done tons of work today. If Amanda wasn't going to stick up for her work, at least he would.

But Charlie still wasn't paying any attention. He pointed to Kyle. "Hey. I heard a rumor about you today." He gave him a sly look.

"About Kyle?" Amanda looked surprised. "What?"

"Apparently, all the girls at Beachwood love Kyle," Charlie answered. "He's everyone's new flavor of the month."

Amanda squinted. "Kyle? Really?"

Charlie snaked his arm around Amanda's waist. "Just don't go stealing Amanda away from me, got it?" He winked, indicating he was kidding. Kyle tried to laugh, but he suddenly felt like someone had put a glass dome around him—he couldn't breathe or move. He looked back and forth from Amanda to Charlie. Something wasn't right. Amanda didn't look intrigued or interested, as Hillary said she would. Instead, she sort of looked . . . confused. Maybe even disgusted. Kyle's chest felt tight. His breathing sped up. She probably knew it was all a lie. And she probably knew *why*.

Suddenly he just wanted out of here . . . before Charlie said anything else. "I'll see you guys later," he blurted out, and burst out the door. He stumbled through the courtyard to an outdoor water fountain. Kyle leaned over it and took a huge drink, and then splashed his face with cold water. His heart was beating very, very fast.

He stood for a long time with his head bent over the fountain, letting the water wash over his nose, chin, and cheeks. When he went back into the rec center to collect his stuff, Amanda and Charlie were gone.

Across the street from the Beachwood Rec Center was the Johnson Memorial Cemetery. It was full of wooded, floral paths; ancient gravestones; and ornate, marble crypts. Tom Foss crouched behind a huge angel statue, his nose tickling and his eyes itching at the smell of the freshly cut flowers a mourner had just put on someone's grave. The graveyard offered him a perfect view of the outside of the rec center. As Kyle went back into the building and the door slammed shut, Foss spoke into the small wireless earpiece he wore.

"He's got the fob," Foss said. "I'm almost sure of it."

"Well, then, you have to get it back," the voice said.

Foss shut his eyes. His botched interaction with

Kyle made him nervous. He hoped his threats would keep Kyle from telling the Trager family that Foss had been there—he needed to keep this as quiet as possible. But he didn't know for certain. What if Kyle told them? What if he had shown them the fob? Stephen Trager worked with software all the time. Could he crack it?

"Can't we just disable it?" Foss asked. "So it doesn't link to anything?"

"But then *we* won't have the link, either," the voice reminded him. "Besides, the fob itself raises some questions, don't you think?"

Suddenly Kyle came back out of the rec center front doors. Foss stood up straighter, his eyes wide. "He's on the move," he whispered.

"Follow him," the voice commanded.

Kyle walked out of the rec center parking lot and down the sidewalk, presumably back toward the Tragers' house. Foss slowly started to tail him, creeping behind tombstones and weaving between the large shrubs that lined the cemetery fence.

"What's he doing?" the voice on the other end asked.

"Nothing," Foss replied. "He's just walking."

"Is he alone?"

"Yes."

"Do you think he has the fob on him right now?" the voice asked.

"I don't know," Foss said. He fumbled around for his pocket binoculars and focused on Kyle's face. Kyle looked troubled and forlorn. *Perhaps he's upset about the fob,* Foss thought. *Perhaps my threats are eating away at him.* He panned down to Kyle's hands, but Kyle didn't seem to be holding anything. And there was no way of telling whether the fob was in his pockets or his back-pack.

"You should approach him," the voice suggested. "Perhaps you could reason with him. Explain that it's to your work e-mail account. That you can't work without it."

"You know as well as I do that he won't buy that," Foss spat, walking right over a bunch of graves. "He's smarter than that. And, besides, he's already seen me. It's a bad idea."

"Then just ambush him," the voice said impatiently. "Do what you have to do. We need it back . . . before it's too late."

"But . . ." Foss trailed off. He'd come smack up against the cemetery's edge. A large, wrought-iron fence separated him from Kyle. Foss looked right and left, and then started to climb it, wedging his foot into the ornate ironwork and pulling himself up. He couldn't let Kyle get away.

"Uh, excuse me?" a voice behind him called.

Foss, now halfway up the fence, turned around. An elderly man in a gray jumpsuit was staring at him. "Yes?" Foss snapped.

"I'm the groundskeeper," the old man said, eyeing Foss suspiciously. "What do you think you're doing?"

"What's going *on*?" the voice on the other end of Foss's phone hissed.

Foss ignored the groundskeeper and continued to climb the fence.

The old man put his hands on his hips. "Get down from there right now, or I'll call the police."

Foss glared at the man, then looked helplessly back at Kyle, who was disappearing down the sidewalk. Finally he shrugged and climbed down.

"What's happening?" the voice asked again.

Foss sighed. "I lost Kyle. I'm going to have to go back and look later tonight."

"Fine," the caller said. "But we're running out of time. If you don't get it soon, we're going to have to take drastic measures."

"I know," Foss said solemnly. "I know."

14. Lessons Learned

Late that same Thursday afternoon, after a stupid after-school detention for being late to science class *yet again*, Josh collapsed against his front door in relief. He had never been so happy to be home.

Somehow, his hangover had managed to last *two days*. Yesterday was a blur, and today seemed even worse. Josh had struggled to get through the day. His head kept spinning and his stomach burbled and even the tiniest noise felt like knives stabbing into his ears and the dimmest light was like headlights shining straight into his brain. Tuesday night's experiment with vodka had done a number on him, and stuff during the past two days had constantly reminded him of it. Yesterday a girl in front of him in English class had been chewing a new flavor of gum called vodka cosmopolitan. She had passed pieces to all her friends, too, so the smell was all around him. Yesterday in math class, a guy in front of him had been wearing a TEN REASONS BEER ROCKS T-shirt, and Josh couldn't stop staring at the frothy beer mug silkscreened on the back. Then today someone in his study hall was wearing the *exact same shirt*, so Josh had to stare at it all over again. They'd even had a pizza party in Algebra II class today, but Josh's stomach was so iffy he didn't dare touch it. And finally, in drivers' ed, the teacher had played them a video about drunk driving—even *watching* kids drink made Josh's head pound. Josh had heard plenty of kids talk almost proudly about being hungover, as if it was fun. What crazy land were they living in?

Or perhaps Josh was some kind of freak. Maybe alcohol affected him more seriously than it affected anyone else in the universe. All in all, this was a little worrying. Either he'd better increase his alcohol tolerance pretty fast, or . . . or what? He wasn't going to be lame and just not drink. So he'd have to suck it up somehow.

Josh dropped his backpack in the foyer and slowly walked up to his room. All he wanted to do was lie on his bed, look at *Playpen's* Miss October, and then sleep for a million years.

When he opened his bedroom door, he froze. Someone had cleaned his room. His clothes were all on hangers instead of all over the floor, the clutter on his desk had been put into neat piles, and his bed had been made. And on top of his quilt, lying jauntily on the pillow like it was a teddy bear, was the bottle of vodka he'd shoved under his bed. There was a little yellow Post-it stuck to the side. *See me,* it said, and was signed *Mom.*

Josh ripped the Post-it off the bottle and crumpled it up. "I'm dead," he whispered, staring at his reflection in the full-length mirror on the back of his door. "I'm dead, I'm dead, I'm dead." He considered climbing out his bedroom window, shimmying down the downspout, and just running away.

"I see you got my note."

Josh turned around. His mother stood in the doorway, her hands on her hips. He opened his mouth, but no sound came out.

"I stayed home because I needed a mental health day," his mother explained. "I caught up on some bills, the laundry, the dishes . . . and, oh, cleaning your room." Her eyes fell to the vodka bottle. "Making martinis, were we? Very James Bond of you."

"Lori put it there," Josh said quickly.

His **781227** mother lowered her chin and gave him a deadly stare. "Right."

"Fine, it was me," Josh said sharply, looking away. "I had a couple shots. No big deal."

"No big *deal*?" his mother demanded.

Josh shrugged. "I just needed to practice for the Monster Mash. Just in case."

"Just in case what? Someone forces a drink down your throat?" his mom scoffed. "Do you have no decision-making abilities of your own?"

"Whatever," Josh said sulkily. He was so not in the mood for the whole don't-succumb-to-peer-pressure lecture.

His mother sat down at his desk. "Do you remember the story I told you about the time your grandma caught me smoking a cigarette?"

"She made you smoke the whole pack," Josh recited.

"That's right. And I never wanted to smoke again." His mother smiled sinisterly, nodding toward the bottle. "I should make you drink the rest of the vodka. What's left of it, anyway."

Josh bugged his eyes out and clutched his stomach. "No way. Believe me, I've learned my lesson."

His mother glanced at the stacks of video games, then picked up *Football for Dummies*, which was lying open on his nightstand. She slowly leafed through the pages, some of which Josh had marked. "You planning on joining the football team, too?"

Josh shrugged. "Maybe."

She laid the book back down and stared at him. "Is

this really Josh Trager? Who are you and what have you done with my son?"

"I'm picking up new interests," Josh insisted toughly. "What's wrong with that?"

"Only that you've talked for *years* about how you would never play football," his mother interrupted him, her voice stern. "Not that I care whether you play football or not. It's your decision. But I'm not stupid. So stop acting like I am."

Josh held up his hands in surrender. "Is it a crime now to have football books in my bedroom? I thought you'd be happy I was actually reading something."

"Football books on your nightstand and a bottle of vodka under your bed," she said slowly. "This is quite a mystery. Do you want to fill me in on the missing connection?"

Josh lowered his eyes. It annoyed him how perceptive his mom was. For once, he wished she wasn't a therapist but some stupid, oblivious, noncommunicative parent who would simply ground him for the vodka and go off to cook dinner. "It's for a girl, all right?" he blurted out. "This beautiful girl, Samantha Jeffries. Kyle and I were at the Halloween store the other day and I tried on this football costume. Samantha saw me and thought I was actually on the team. And I sort of . . . didn't correct her."

"I see." His mother crossed and uncrossed her legs. "So you're brushing up on football terms to perpetuate the lie."

"That's one way of putting it," Josh muttered.

"And you're practicing drinking because . . . what? All football players drink?"

"Maybe," Josh mumbled.

His mother reached her hand out and put it on Josh's

knee. "Why are you pretending to be someone else?"

Josh wrenched his knee away. "Because. I have to."

"You've never done that for a girl before."

Josh flung himself backward on the bed. "But this is Samantha *Jeffries*, Mom. The most popular girl in Seattle. She's a model! Every guy, like, *fantasizes* about her! If I blow this, I'll probably never have an opportunity to speak to her ever again!"

"Why don't you think she'd like you for who you are?"

Josh stuffed his face into his pillow and curled his toes. "She just won't, all right?"

They sat there for a while in silence. Josh breathed in and out, the pillowcase right up next to his mouth. He sat up and stared at his mom defeatedly. "So I'm grounded, right? No Mash for me?"

His mom thought for a moment. "Oh, you're definitely grounded . . . but you can go to the Mash. But I want you to tell this girl the truth—that you're not a football player."

Josh's eyes widened. "I'll take staying home instead."

"Too bad." His mother pushed her blond hair behind her ears. "What are you so afraid of, anyway? If this girl truly likes you, she won't care that you don't play football." She put a finger to her lips. "Or maybe it's *easier* to pretend to be someone else instead of yourself. Because that way, if she rejects you, she's not really turning *you* down but rather your football player alter ego."

Josh shut his eyes. "Stop it with the analysis, Dr. Freud. I *get it*."

"Good." She patted his arm. "Oh, and I guess this goes without saying, but if I detect even the tiniest bit of alcohol on your breath when you come home from the Mash, you're not leaving this house again until you're eighteen."

"I know, I know," Josh groaned.

Suddenly they heard Josh's father's voice at the foot of the stairs. "Nicole?" he called. "Nicole? Where are you?" He sounded alarmed.

Josh and his mom stood up. "What is it?" she asked in response, walking into the hall. Josh followed.

His father was in the foyer, craning his neck up at them. "There's someone skulking around by our shed," he said. "He seems suspicious."

"What should we do?" Josh's mother cried.

"Get the phone," his father urged. "Call the neighborhood patrolman."

Lori wandered into the hall, holding her iPod in one hand and her cell phone in the other. "What's going on?"

"There's a strange man in the yard outside," her mother said. She walked quickly into her bedroom and emerged with the cordless phone.

"What are we going to do?" Lori shrieked.

"Let's all just stay calm," Mr. Trager said. "There's no need to panic."

Josh returned to his bedroom, which faced the back of the house. Sure enough, he could see a man hovering by the garden near the shed. He was poking through the rosebushes as if he'd lost something.

"Where's Kyle?" Stephen called from downstairs. "Are we all inside?"

"I'm here," Kyle said, emerging from his downstairs bedroom. He had been lying in his bathtub, thinking about Operation Make Her Jealous and Amanda. "What's going on?"

"There's someone in our backyard," Stephen explained, "near the shed."

Kyle's heart started to speed up. He watched as Stephen walked angrily toward the back door. "What are you doing?" Kyle asked.

"I'm going to try and scare him off," Stephen said over his shoulder.

Kyle's eyes widened. "No!" he cried. "That could be dangerous!"

Stephen looked at him strangely, then turned away. "I can handle it. Maybe he doesn't realize we're home." He rolled his shoulders back, shook out his arms, and turned on the porch light.

Upstairs, Josh watched as the porch light snapped on and the guy by the shed froze. Then he sprang into action, leaping out of the bushes, across the yard, and into the shadows. "He's on the move!" Josh called down the stairs.

By the time the rest of the family had run upstairs to Josh's room, the intruder was gone. "Did you get a good look at him?" his mom asked.

Josh shook his head. "He had on a hooded sweat-shirt. And he was five ten, maybe five eleven. That's all I got."

Kyle reached into his pocket and curled his palm around the key fob. He wasn't sure what to do.

"Did you get through to the police?" Stephen asked Nicole.

"I didn't call yet," Nicole answered.

"Maybe we should anyway," Lori said.

Nicole looked around at all of them. "Have any of you seen someone skulking around the house recently?"

Josh shrugged. "Nope."

"Not that I'm aware of," Lori seconded.

Nicole's eyes landed on Kyle. He ran his tongue over his teeth. If he told the truth now, it would be a huge deal—they would be angry with him because he hadn't said anything before. And . . . Foss had told him not to, right? He didn't want anyone to get hurt. "I haven't seen anyone," he said in a small voice.

Josh sat down on his bed. "He was rooting around those bushes as if he'd lost something there. It was freaky."

"What could he be looking for?" Nicole wondered.

Kyle's face was positively burning. He kept his eyes glued to Josh's striped carpet.

"It's probably drugs," Stephen concluded. "Addicts do some pretty bizarre things."

"True," Nicole said.

"Still," Lori said, running her hand through her hair. "I'm scared."

"It'll be okay," Nicole said quickly.

They all stood there for another moment, letting the situation sink in. "I'm going to start dinner," Nicole finally said. "Lori, do you want to help me?"

"Sure," Lori said.

"I'll help, too," Josh agreed.

Kyle watched as the family walked down the stairs together. *They must feel so frightened,* he thought. And it was all because of him. Because he'd chosen to hide what he knew.

He slowly walked downstairs into his bedroom and sat down on the edge of his tub. After a moment, he took the key fob out of his pocket and held it in his palm. He was growing more and more certain that this was what Foss was looking for. Part of him wanted to leave the fob in the dirt by the rosebushes, so that if Foss came again, he could just take it.

But something deep inside him resisted. The fob had something to do with him. Kyle wasn't sure how he knew, he just . . . did. Perhaps it unlocked something about Kyle himself. Something . . . dangerous, just as Foss said. Kyle stared at the fob, looking for any details he might have missed. The numbers changed again. 239075. 548701. 997452. They were meaningless. He turned the fob over, hoping to find a telltale crack, a secret code carved into the side of the device, a miniature computer chip, anything. But the back was red plastic, smooth and blank. Completely and frustratingly anonymous.

Tom Foss bolted through the bushes and scrambled into his truck. That was entirely too close. Just as he put his key into the ignition, he noticed something on the wireless receiver he had sitting on the passenger seat. The receiver picked up the feed from the camera Foss had installed in the Kyle's bedroom weeks ago, way before this key fob mess even happened. He had installed several cameras in the house after picking the locks on a day all the Tragers were out. Right now, Kyle was right in the camera's view. He sat on the edge of his tub, looking at something. At first, Foss couldn't tell what it was, but then Kyle moved his head away, revealing something in his palm.

The *fob*.

Foss's mouth fell open. He watched as Kyle turned the fob over and over in his hands. It was so close . . . and yet so far away. Foss couldn't go back for it now. The Tragers were on high alert—he'd seen the younger boy in his bedroom window and the father at the back door. They may have even called the cops.

No, he had to do this very, very carefully. But he had to make his move soon.

15. Smile
for the Cameras

Lori stood at her parents' bedroom bureau mirror, watching her mother position a long, straight blond wig on her head. Her mother also wore a long paisley dress, hideous brown sandals, and a billion beaded necklaces. She patted her head and turned around for Lori to see. "What do you think?" she asked. "Is this costume *costumey* enough?"

Lori raised her eyebrows. It was Saturday, Halloween night, and her parents were going to a costume party down the street. Her mom and dad had decided to dress as hippies, and with the wig on her head, her mom looked like the vegan girls at her school who protested biology dissections, took nothing but art classes, and didn't shower often. "Peace, Mom," Lori finally said. "Make love, not war."

Her father stepped out of the bathroom. Lori burst out laughing. He wore a long-haired wig, too; pink-tinted wire-rimmed glasses; a tie-dyed shirt; baggy jeans; and sandals. He looked at his wife and grinned. "You look exactly like you did when I met you."

"And that's a *good* thing?" Lori asked.

"Can you believe we found most of this stuff in our closets?" her mother crowed, stretching her arms out and admiring her paisley dress. "And I'm astounded this still fits!"

"It's a tent," Lori pointed out. "Of course it's going to fit."

Her father trundled back into the bathroom, and her mom went to work doing her makeup. Halfway finished with one eye, she paused and gazed at Lori. "Don't you need to get dressed for the Mash?" she asked, appraising Lori's outfit of a ripped T-shirt, plaid pajama pants, and white-and-black cow-shaped slippers. "Hillary's going to be here any minute. Josh and Kyle are already changing."

Lori shrugged. She thought about the black, skimpy costume hanging in her closet. Before the run-in with Declan Wednesday, she'd broken down and bought a sexy cat outfit—a compromise for Hillary, who still wanted her to go as slutty Tinker Bell. "You know what? I'm just not feeling it tonight. I think I'm going to stay in." She tried to say it casually, like the idea had just come to her.

Her mother whirled around. "But you love the Monster Mash. You've gone every year."

Lori shrugged. "I need the night off."

Her mother stared at her, but Lori wouldn't give her the satisfaction of staring back. She wasn't about to explain this. It was bad enough that she had broken down in front of Kyle. All she wanted to do was crawl into bed, go to sleep, and wake up five years later—high school would be over, Declan a mere memory, and she would be happy and well-adjusted and probably have tons of boys falling all over her.

"Do you want to come to the party with us?" her mother asked.

Lori's mouth dropped open. "Ew! No!"

Her mother glanced at her. "It'll be fun."

Lori slumped back on her mom's bed, an itchy,

clammy feeling welling over her. The last thing she wanted was her mom's pity. "Thanks but no thanks. I don't do geriatric parties."

"Not nice." Her mom sounded hurt. "It's just . . . I'm not sure if I want you here alone with that strange man running around."

"I'll be fine," Lori groaned. "It's Halloween night. Why would that guy be running around with tons of people out trick-or-treating? And, anyway, you're going to be right down the street. I'll call if anything happens."

"Do you want to hand out candy?" her mother asked. When she noticed Lori's appalled expression, she quickly nodded. "Okay. That's fine. We'll just put a basket out for the kids. No problem."

Her mother looked like she was about to ask Lori another prying question when the doorbell rang. Lori jumped up. "I bet that's Hillary," she said, darting out of the room, eager for any excuse to get away.

In the hall, she practically bumped smack into Kyle and Josh. They were both dressed up for the Monster Mash—Josh in a Zorro costume he ended up buying at a store called Satan's Workshop, Kyle in his Prince Charming outfit. "Whoa," Lori said. "You two look like freaks."

"No, they look fabulous!" Nicole cried, following Lori out in the hall. "My goodness! Kyle! You're a vision in purple!"

"Thanks." Kyle itched under the ruff of his royal-purple puffy shirt. With his lavender vest, dark plum pants, and matching dark purple shoes, he felt a bit grapelike. There were all sorts of medals on his vest, a sword on his hip, and a silvery crown on his head. He didn't look like himself tonight, but he wasn't sure he looked like a prince either.

The bell rang again. Kyle and Nicole walked down the stairs and opened the door. Hillary leaned seductively against the doorjamb, reapplying a coat of dark red lipstick. She had piled her hair atop her head and nestled a tiara in her honey-colored ringlets. She wore so much eye makeup and blush, she looked a bit airbrushed. Hillary's purple-sequined dress was backless, tight across the chest, and the skirt ended barely on her thighs.

"Kyle!" Hillary chirped. "You look awesome!"

"T-thanks," Kyle stammered.

"And Hillary," Nicole said slowly, a startled expression on her face. "You look—"

"I know. I look *amazing*," Hillary interrupted. She spun around a little for them. Earlier today, Nicole and Kyle had watched the *Cinderella* Disney movie together, just so Kyle had some idea who Prince Charming *was*. If someone—the evil sisters, perhaps—had forced the Cinderella in the film to wear Hillary's dress, Kyle was pretty sure she would have hidden in her pumpkin coach all night, embarrassed that someone might get the wrong idea about her.

"And how do I look?" Josh clomped down the stairs and drew a Zorro Z in the air close to Hillary's face.

"Nothing like Antonio Banderas," Hillary said quickly, rolling her eyes.

"Let's get some pictures." Nicole held a digital camera up to her face and instructed Hillary, Kyle, and Josh to all stand together. Kyle smiled as the flash went off. Then Nicole and Stephen posed next to Kyle and Josh, and Hillary took their picture.

"Where's Lori?" Hillary asked. She walked to the foot of the stairs. "Oh, Kitty Cat! Get your butt down here!" She turned to the others. "She didn't put on that dead witch costume, did she? I'll kill her if she did."

Lori stood at the top of the stairs, her arms crossed over her T-shirt. Her pajama pants bottoms scraped the carpet. "I'm not going."

Hillary's mouth fell open. *"What?"*

Lori shrugged, her hair falling over her face. "I'm not going, okay? I don't feel like it."

Hillary let out a small, confused squeak. Lori widened her eyes, to indicate she didn't want to talk about it right now. Hillary finally shrugged. "I'll text you once we're in the car," she mouthed. Lori made a mental note to turn her cell phone off.

"I'll be fine," Lori said loudly. "I just need to decompress and chill." Suddenly a horrible image flashed in front of her head—somewhere, right now, Declan was standing on a girl's front porch, dressed up in a Halloween costume, ready to take her to the Mash. Her parents were probably taking pictures of them, and Declan was probably smiling, without a care in the world.

Lori felt her cheeks start to flush. Her eyes felt itchy and wet and her throat tickled. "See you guys later," she blurted out, turning around and running down the hall.

There was an awkward silence. "Should I talk to her?" Nicole asked quietly.

"You should probably just leave her be," Hillary advised.

Kyle looked up the stairs, thinking about how her face had crumpled after her run-in with Declan. He wished there was something he could do.

Nicole looked like she really wanted to go upstairs

but was restraining herself. Finally she turned to Hillary and Kyle. "Well. You two have a great time. Be good, Kyle. And you *definitely* be good, Josh. Remember what we talked about?"

"Yeah, yeah," Josh mumbled. Admit to beautiful and amazing Samantha Jeffries that he wasn't a football player. He was trying his best to accidentally forget.

"Hang on," Hillary said. "We can't leave without putting these on." She held two silver-white masks, one for her and one for Kyle. Kyle walked over to the mirror and slipped it over his face. The mask covered his nose, making his face unrecognizable.

"I'm hidden," he said quietly to his reflection.

"Come on, Prince," Hillary said, taking Kyle's arm and gesturing to her car, which was parked at the curb. "Our carriage awaits."

Kyle followed her out the door, waving good-bye to Josh, who was getting a ride with his friend Doug. But as they walked down the front steps, Kyle felt the familiar tingling sensation at the back of his neck. He stopped short. *Someone was here.*

He glanced around the side of the house but didn't see anyone. Maybe it was a false alarm. He slipped his hand into his pocket and felt for the key fob. He wasn't sure why he'd decided to bring it with him tonight. He just had a feeling that he should.

Meanwhile, in a small, dark room across town, Tom Foss sat at his desk, watching a wall of monitors. Each fuzzy, black-and-white image was of a different room in a house. There was a kitchen, a master bedroom, a computer room, a back porch, a front porch, and another bedroom.

A bedroom that had a tub for a bed.

Foss ran his hand through his hair, staring at the clump of costumed people in the Tragers' foyer. After posing for pictures, three teenagers bounded out the door. Not fifteen minutes later, the parents left, too. He clicked over to the monitor that showed Kyle's empty bedroom. He zeroed in on Kyle's desk, and then panned to his carpet, then to Kyle's tub. Was the fob in there, or had Kyle taken it with him?

Foss's phone rang. He looked at the screen, raised an eyebrow, and picked up. "Are we doing this tonight?" the voice on the other end asked.

"I don't know," Foss said.

The voice grumbled. "The longer Kyle has the fob, the more dangerous it is for us. He's going to uncover its secret sooner or later. And we don't want him poking around, asking questions."

Foss stared at the empty rooms on the video monitors. "I think you're right. Tonight's the night."

"Wait until it gets a little darker," the voice advised, "and then go in."

"Got it," Foss answered, then hung up.

16. You Can Run...

O nly minutes later, Hillary's car pulled up to the familiar circular entrance of the Beachwood Rec Center. Kyle and Hillary got out and walked to the long line of kids waiting to get in. There was a chill in the air, and the breeze smelled like burning leaves. The fat, full, yellow moon shone down on all the spiderwebs Kyle and Amanda had put up outside the front entrance.

"Ew," Hillary shrieked, pointing at a large, silky, fake spider Kyle had placed in the middle of one of the webs. "Gross-ola."

Kids dressed as gorillas, owls, and axe-wielding murderers stood in front of them, waiting to get into the party. Kyle started to jiggle up and down with anticipation. He felt sort of invincible in his mask, like he was capable of anything. People were looking at him suspiciously, as if they couldn't quite figure out who he was. Perhaps he *was* truly hidden.

Hillary grabbed his arm. "Operation Make Her Jealous is going to totally work, so stop fidgeting like you've got bugs in your boxers." Kyle stood still. "By the end of the night, *you're* going to be her Prince Charming, not Charlie," Hillary went on. "But we're really going to have to lay it on thick tonight."

"How?" Kyle whispered back.

"We have to act like the perfect couple," Hillary explained. "Just follow my lead, okay?"

They walked through the familiar grand entrance.

The rec center seemed different tonight, spooky and otherworldly. Kids in all sorts of costumes filled the room. They mingled in groups of threes and fours, admiring one another's outfits. The orange lights Kyle had installed yesterday illuminated the drinks and snacks tables; the pathways to the bathrooms; and large statues of mummies, goblins, and witches Amanda had rented from a theater prop store. There was a long line to tour the haunted house, and a three-piece rock band wailed away onstage. Off to the right was the mural he and Amanda had spent all week painting. The moon seemed to glow. The ghosts rose from the graves. The giant, howling wolf looked so lifelike, a girl dressed as an elf reached out and touched it to make sure it wasn't real.

Kyle looked around for Amanda, wanting to see what she thought of the mural, too. When he noticed her standing by one of the bigfoot statues, his heart leaped. Amanda wore a fitted bodice; a knee-length skirt; and black, knee-high boots. Her hair was stuffed into a beret and she wore dark red lipstick. Kyle had never seen Amanda in red lipstick before. She looked dangerous.

Kyle was about to wave to her when Hillary caught his arm.

"What do you think you're doing?" she said through clenched teeth.

"Saying hi?" Kyle answered.

Hillary shook her head and steered him in the opposite direction. "No way. You can't talk to her. That's the *point*. You have to pretend you're totally into me."

Kyle's mouth dropped open. "I can't talk to her? You didn't tell me that."

Hillary shrugged. "I guess I forgot." She pointed to Kyle's mask. "And take that off, too. You look lame."

"But I thought we were supposed to wear masks," Kyle protested.

"Only to get in," Hillary pointed out. She waved her arm around the room. "Do you see anyone *else* in a mask?"

Kyle had to admit that he didn't.

Then Hillary's eyes lit up. She pointed across the room. "Look! Let's get our picture taken!"

Before Kyle could respond, Hillary grabbed his hand and dragged him toward a large banner in the corner that said MONSTER MASH COMMEMORATIVE PHOTOS. A photographer sat on a stool, his camera pointed at a graveyard backdrop. Two kids, one dressed as a witch and the other as a prisoner, walked in front of the backdrop and posed. "Say Satan!" the photographer instructed. The two kids smiled.

Kyle looked around the room again. Amanda was now standing next to Charlie, near the drinks table. Charlie was dressed in a pinstriped suit. A cigar hung out of his mouth, and he was holding a fake pistol and a bag of money. Kyle wondered who Amanda and Charlie were supposed to be.

Hillary tilted Kyle's chin away from them and back to her. "Pay attention to *me*, Kyle," she sang hypnotically. "Otherwise, this isn't going to work."

It was finally Kyle and Hillary's turn to get their picture taken. They stood in front of the backdrop, and Kyle stared into the camera lens. "Say Beelzebub!" the photographer crowed. Kyle dutifully tried to smile, but he wasn't sure his mouth was responding. At the last second, Hillary turned her face and gave Kyle a huge, wet kiss on his cheek. The flash went off. Then Hillary tilted Kyle's chin toward her and gave him an enormous kiss right on his lips.

"Whoa!" someone in the line cried.

"Hot!" someone else said.

Hillary's mouth was warm and firm and tasted like breath mints. Kyle could feel his heart pounding through his ears, the top of his head, and even his feet. The flash went off again, and all he saw for a few seconds were spots. When his vision cleared, he looked across the room for Amanda again. She was still standing there with Charlie, talking to a bunch of kids. He hoped she hadn't seen Hillary kissing him.

The band started to play a slow song, and all the couples bustled out to the dance floor. Hillary took his hand. "Time to dance."

Kyle was beginning to feel a bit like a puppet, guided by Hillary's every movement. They walked into the very center of the dance floor. All around them, couples swayed from side to side to the music. Kyle thought again of Amanda's dancing lesson. *This is the way people dance when they really like each other,* she'd said. *"It's supposed to be romantic."*

Hillary wasn't shy about wrapping her arms around Kyle's neck and encouraging him to put his arms a little bit lower on her back. "You have to seem like you want me just a little," Hillary teased him. She giggled. "We should've had a couple shots in the car to loosen you up."

Kyle felt a tap on his shoulder. He gasped, thinking it might be Amanda, but it was a small, violet-eyed girl wearing rabbit ears and a tail. She and a large, green-faced Frankenstein were dancing right next to them. The girl pointed to Kyle and Hillary. "You guys look so cute together."

"Thanks, Lindsay," Hillary said proudly, giving Kyle a little peck on the cheek.

"How long have you been going out?" Lindsay asked.

"Oh, not long," Hillary said, "but we're *madly* in love."

She wrapped her arms tighter around Kyle. Kyle couldn't do anything but stand there, feeling a bit stunned. He felt Hillary's pointy heel grinding into his foot. "Say *something*," she whispered into Kyle's ear. "Do it for Amanda."

Kyle sighed. "We're totally in love," he blurted out robotically. He shut his eyes and went to kiss Hillary on the cheek, but somehow missed and got her nose.

"You guys are adorable," Lindsay cooed approvingly.

As soon as the other couple turned away, Kyle let out the breath he had been holding for what seemed like forever. He felt dizzy and hot, as if someone had jacked up the heat. He wasn't sure how much longer he could pretend like this.

By the time they got in line for the haunted house, Hillary had practically undressed Kyle on the dance floor, done a weird grinding dance near the stage, smacked his butt, and talked about how in love they were to six different people. He felt drained and was growing more and more uncomfortable by the second. However, Hillary's tactics were definitely working—a lot of girls stared at Kyle curiously, as if they were seeing him for the very first time.

Kyle sort of felt like Hillary had somehow transformed him into someone else. Kyle kept searching the room for Amanda, but she seemed to have vanished—Kyle hadn't seen her at all since he'd had his picture taken.

The line for the haunted house wasn't very long, and soon they were walking up the house's creaky wooden steps. Booing ghosts, howling wolves, and cackling witches all called to them as they went through the cobwebbed front door.

Inside, it was pitch-black. All Kyle could hear was Hillary's sharp, ragged breathing. When another ghost moaned, Hillary grabbed Kyle's arm.

"Are you okay?" he asked quietly.

"I'm fine," Hillary said quickly.

They took a tentative step toward a dim lightbulb at the back of the house. Suddenly some lights flashed. A clap of thunder sounded. Something laughed menacingly from a dark corner. Kyle saw a flock of bats emerge from the corner. "Duck!" he yelled, pulling Hillary to the ground. Hillary let out a shrill shriek and curled up into a ball on the floor. The bats mechanically fluttered by them, disappearing into a notch in the wall.

They slowly stood back up and took another step forward, when suddenly a ratty old living room chair lit up. A rotted-looking corpse sat slumped in the chair. The hairs on the back of Kyle's neck stood. He could sense something was about to happen. Kyle took a step back, pulling Hillary with him. Sure enough, the corpse leaped off the chair, reaching its arms for them. Hillary screamed again, burying her head in Kyle's chest like she was going to burst into sobs. "It's okay, it's okay," he murmured.

The dummy retracted back to his seat. Hillary breathed heavily. "How do you know that all this stuff is going to happen?" she asked. "Did you work on the haunted house?"

"No," Kyle whispered. He thought for a moment. "I

don't know how I know it's going to happen. I just . . . do." He looked ahead. The dim bulb at the back of the building was getting closer. "We're almost through this," he said. "Do you want to keep going?"

"I guess so," Hillary said nervously.

They took a few more steps forward. Another swarm of bats dove for them, but Kyle told Hillary to duck just in time. Then he pulled Hillary away just before a spider could scuttle across her feet. When they were almost at the exit, Kyle sensed something else. *Someone is watching us*, he thought. His neck tingled. His chest tightened. He closed his eyes and tried to picture whatever spooky thing was next, just as he'd predicted the spiders, the bats, and all the other threats. This time, however, all he saw was Tom Foss's face.

Kyle's eyes snapped open. "No," he whispered. Was it possible that Foss was . . . here? Had he found Kyle, even though Kyle was in costume?

Kyle's heart sped up. He curled his fingers around the fob. He could just make out a pair of eyes staring at them from the dark corner. As the figure rose, Kyle reacted. He let out a frustrated groan, wrapped his hands around Foss's neck and squeezed. Hillary screamed.

But something didn't feel right. Foss's neck felt soft—*too* soft. Kyle couldn't feel tendons and bone underneath skin but rather some sort of fluffy padding. The light from the exit shone in, and Kyle stepped away. It wasn't Foss at all, just another dummy. Kyle could see the dents in its neck from where he'd squeezed. Its head sagged at an unnatural angle, and there was a bit of stuffing seeping out its ear.

A few seconds of silence passed. Kyle felt his heart slowing down. Hillary touched his arm. "What was that all about?" she asked, sounding a little weirded out.

"I don't know," Kyle said quietly. The dummy settled back into the corner, ready to scare the next couple. It might not have been Foss this time, but Kyle still had a terrible feeling that Foss was close.

Too close.

17. The Truth Will Come Out

Josh sat on the roof of the rec center, watching as his friends Doug and Robbie flirted with girls who weren't nearly as smoking hot as Samantha Jeffries was. His stomach was jumping like it was on fire, and he kept nervously running his hands over the big Z that was emblazoned across his chest. Doug had already teased Josh about it, saying it sort of looked like he was feeling himself up.

"So, Josh, where is she?" asked Robbie, who was dressed as an executioner. "I thought she'd be here by now."

Josh crossed his arms over his chest. He'd bragged about Samantha to his friends, and they totally didn't believe a word of it. "She's coming. I promise."

"You know, I heard that girl's psycho," Doug said, itching under his Chewbacca mask. "She's like a super-stalker. And she keeps her boyfriends on a really short leash."

Josh shrugged, inhaling the intoxicating smell of burning leaves, the Mash apple cider, and someone's cigarette. "I am perfectly fine with being on Samantha Jeffries's leash."

"Dude, I heard something about that, too," Robbie piped in. "She makes guys her personal slaves."

"Again." Josh raised his arms in indifference. "Not a problem."

"My brother has a friend who went out with her last year," Doug said. "She went loco on him one night because he didn't call her back at *exactly* the time she asked him to. She's one of *those* girls."

Josh rolled his eyes. They were just jealous.

Suddenly a shadow loomed above him. "Josh?"

He looked up. *Samantha.* The roof's floodlights created an ethereal halo around her head. Samantha was dressed as a Vegas showgirl, clad in a sequined body suit, a huge feathered headdress, and white, knee-high boots. Her long blond hair fell to her shoulders.

"Sexy," Doug said. Amazingly he and Robbie moved away to give Josh a bit of privacy.

"Hi." Josh looked into Samantha's eyes. "I thought maybe you weren't coming."

Samantha sat down next to him. "My friend's car broke down on the side of the road. It was *so* horrible, although we had some rum while we were waiting." When she leaned over to pet Josh's arm, he could smell the hot, acrid smell of rum on her breath.

"That's cool," Josh said. "About the rum, I mean."

"Damn right." Samantha grinned. Then she looked Josh over. "So how are you feeling?"

Josh raised a curious eyebrow.

"Your knee injury," Samantha pointed out. She bit her lip flirtatiously. "I hope you can still dance."

Josh took a deep breath. This was definitely the moment to tell her. It would be so easy, just a few simple words: *I don't have a knee injury. And I'm not a football player.* The words welled up inside him, but he couldn't quite get them to come out of his mouth. Samantha was looking at him so adoringly. How many times had he dreamed about her? How many guys would *kill* to be with her right now? And what guy took his mom's advice, anyway?

"It's feeling pretty good tonight," he finally mustered. "All that rest must've paid off."

"Good." Samantha wrapped her arm around Josh. Her limbs were wobbly, as if all her bones had been removed. Josh wondered just how much rum she'd drunk in the car. "So. I'm drinking with a couple of my friends in the parking lot. Wanna come?" She nudged him. "I know how much you like tequila."

Josh's stomach turned, but he stood up. "Sure."

Samantha grinned. "Awesome."

He followed Samantha down the stairs. As she took his hand and they wound around the other partiers, he felt amazingly self-confident. *Look at me!* he wanted to scream at everyone. *I'm with Samantha Jeffries! The hottest girl alive!*

At the very back of the rec center parking lot were three girls and two guys, presumably from Samantha's school. The girls were all dressed as showgirls, too, and the guys were dressed as rappers. They sat on the pavement with their knees curled into their chests. In the middle of their circle was a large paper bag. Josh assumed the tequila bottle was inside.

"Hey, guys," Samantha said in a loud voice. She put her arm around Josh. "This is Josh, the hottest guy at Beachwood."

The hottest guy at Beachwood? Josh's insides fluttered. Well, then. This night was just getting better and better.

"Hey, Josh," everyone said.

"He plays on the football team," Samantha explained.

"Really?" A brunette showgirl cocked her head. "What position?"

"Uh, quarterback," Josh said, remembering he'd told Samantha that the day they'd met.

"My brother's best friend plays tight end for Beachwood," the brunette said. "Trevor Gates?"

"Uh, yeah," Josh said, "sure." He vaguely knew who Trevor was. He hoped to God Trevor wasn't *here*.

"I'll have to tell him I met you," the brunette said, her eyes twinkling.

Josh gritted his teeth. "Please don't," he muttered quietly.

"Hey, Josh?" Samantha interrupted. She fluttered her eyelashes. "Do you think you could go get me a diet Sprite at the drinks table inside? I totally need a mixer whenever I drink tequila."

"Sure," Josh said, getting up.

Samantha gave him a winning smile and a kiss on the cheek. He caught a whiff of the rum on her breath again, but her face smelled like Noxema and some sort of intoxicating flower. "Thanks so much," she whispered seductively in his ear.

But when he came back with a big red plastic cup and Samantha tasted it, she shook her head. "This isn't diet."

"They didn't have diet," Josh explained. "I looked through all the bottles. So I just got you regular Sprite."

"I hate regular," Samantha proclaimed, pursing her lips angrily. "I need diet." She shrugged. "Could you run out to the 7-Eleven and get me a bottle?"

Josh stared at her. "Are you serious?" It wasn't like 7-Eleven was *close*.

Samantha widened her giant blue eyes. "You want me to have fun tonight, don't you?"

Aren't you having fun already? Josh wanted to ask. "I don't think a little non-diet Sprite is going to kill you," he said instead.

Josh noticed Samantha's friends exchange a tiny, worried look.

Samantha glowered at him. "Josh," she said in a warning tone. "I need this. Okay? So go get it for me."

Josh didn't know what else to do but stand up, sigh, and agree. He walked across the parking lot, trying to press down his feelings of annoyance. Okay, so Samantha was a little demanding. And she was a bit of a megapartier. So what? He had to keep thinking about later—when they'd be making out. Right? A little bit of crazy-girl syndrome was totally worth it.

As he rounded the corner, he noticed a blue Porta Potti. He decided that while he was here, he might as well go. Josh pushed the plastic door open, held his breath to ward off the stink, and went inside. When he came back out, he was surprised to see Samantha standing in front of the bathroom, hands on her hips, swaying back and forth crookedly.

She seemed surprised. "Josh! What are you doing here?"

Josh smiled crookedly. "Peeing?"

"Did you get my Sprite?"

"Not yet," Josh said. "Do you want to go get it with me? We could take a fun little walk."

She moved closer, and Josh noticed that her eyes seemed unfocused. She bumped into him, then giggled. "So can I let you in on a little secret?" she asked, batting her eyelashes. She wound her hand around Josh's wrist. "I'm kind of wasted."

"That's okay," Josh said quickly. "Let's walk it off a little."

"I'd rather make out," Samantha said bluntly. "With you."

Josh's heart pounded. He wasn't going to say no to that.

But to Josh's horror, Samantha pulled him back into the toilet. "We're going to make out in *here*?" he shrieked.

"Why not?" Samantha slurred. "It's so private."

"But . . ." Josh didn't know what else to do but follow her. He considered holding his nose, but then didn't—he'd look like Captain Dork. The door slammed shut. He felt Samantha's hand curl around his. Then, all of a sudden, Samantha leaned over the toilet and threw up. Josh pressed himself up against the wall, frozen. Samantha retched for what seemed like hours. Josh didn't know whether to laugh or cry. Finally she let out a groan and stood up. She looked at Josh blearily and then smiled.

"Are you . . . okay?" he asked, trying not to breathe.

"Sure," she said breezily. "Perfect."

She took Josh's hand, banged out of the Porta Potti, and stumbled onto the lawn. She pulled Josh down with her. Josh tumbled down, burying his nose in the grass. Next to the Porta Potti, the superfertilized lawn smelled delicious.

"You're cute, Josh," Samantha slurred.

"You are, too," Josh squeaked, his heart beating fast.

Their faces were very close. For a while, neither said anything. Josh felt his arms shake. Here was his big moment, and he had no idea what to do. He should kiss Samantha. Maybe try to hook up with her. But the only thing he could think of was how badly her breath stank. And the horrible noises she'd just made. To be honest, he felt supremely grossed out.

Samantha cocked her head. "So now that I told you a secret, are you going to tell me one, too?"

"Is that how this game works?" Josh asked, blinking at Samantha in the darkness.

"Uh-huh," Samantha said.

Josh hesitated. Here was moment number two. If Samantha was able to act like an idiot around him—she'd *thrown up* while he was standing right there—maybe he *could* show her who he really was. Maybe it wouldn't matter at all. And they were boyfriend and girlfriend, right? Officially.

He took a deep breath. "Well, actually . . . I'm not really a football player. I lied."

Silence. For a second, Josh worried that Samantha had passed out. Then she let out a huge, disgusted breath. "*What?*" she said sharply.

Josh paused. *Uh-oh.*

Samantha stood up unsteadily. She put her hands on her hips and glared at Josh. "If you're not a football player, then what are you?"

"I'm . . . just a guy, I guess."

Samantha made a small, horrified squeak. She looked Josh up and down and shook her head. "God, I should've known," she spat. "You *seemed* a little too small to be on the team."

With that, she stumbled back toward her friends. Josh watched her go, too stunned to follow. When she was almost at the circle of kids, Samantha's feet tangled up underneath her, and she took a massive header onto the pavement. The girls tried to help her up, but she waved them off, saying she was fine.

Maybe it was better Josh had ended it when he did.

He walked back into the party, feeling disappointed

and empty. His big chance of a lifetime had been thrown away. Maybe he should have handled it differently. Maybe he shouldn't have told the truth.

As he was walking past the dance floor, someone grabbed his arm. Josh turned, expecting to see Samantha, but to his surprise, it was a petite brunette girl dressed as Lara Croft from *Tomb Raider*—she had on a silvery bodysuit, a gun holster, and high black boots. Her hair was slicked back in a ponytail, and she looked like she was ready to kick some butt.

"Josh Trager?" the girl asked. She blinked, then slowly smiled. "Do you remember me?"

Josh blinked. It was Ashleigh Redmond, the hot tub girl. Josh hadn't seen her since Jeff Preston's party, when Mrs. Preston pulled her out of the tub and kicked Josh out. "Sure I do," he said. "Had any more hot tub incidents lately?"

"Nah," Ashleigh said. "I was grounded for*ever* after that." She giggled. "It was fun, though, wasn't it?"

"Totally," Josh said.

Ashleigh cocked her head. "I heard this blond girl talking about you about a little while ago. She said you played Beachwood football. Is that true?"

"Nah," Josh said immediately, wondering who else Samantha had told. "I suck at football. Whoever that is has me mixed up with someone else."

"Cool." Ashleigh seemed relieved. "I think football players are meatheads, anyway."

"And so are the girls who like them." Josh laughed. He linked his arm with hers and they bounded away.

18. Facing the Music

A half hour later, Hillary had to go to the bathroom, and Kyle slumped down on one of the spiderweb-covered velvet couches that lined the room. He wanted to go home. Pretending to be Hillary's boyfriend seemed to suck some sort of major life force out of him. He felt as if he'd run a marathon and hadn't drunk any water or eaten any food for days. Plus he still felt shaken by what had happened in the haunted house.

A short, dark-haired freshman girl dressed as a witch—if witches wore hot pants and bikini tops—stood above him. "Are you Kyle?" she asked shyly.

"Yes," Kyle said.

The girl looked excited. "Can I kiss your cheek?" she squeaked. "I heard kissing you will give me magical powers."

Kyle stared at her. Hillary's rumors had seemingly taken on a life of their own. This was the third freshman girl who had come up to him with a crazy request. "Um . . ." he started, but the girl grabbed his face anyway and pressed her lips to his cheek. She squealed with glee, then skipped away. Kyle felt baffled. Did all rumors get as out of control as this? Were there rumors about him at his old school, the one he'd gone to in his past life?

The band abruptly stopped; the lights dimmed to a spooky, orangish haze; and a rotund, bald man strolled onto the stage and gazed out at the students. It was Mr.

Parsons, the principal at Fox High, one of the neighboring high schools, and the chairman of the Monster Mash planning committee. "Welcome to the seventeenth annual Monster Mash. It's time for our Halloween karaoke contest!" he boomed.

The room rippled with applause. Kyle looked around for Hillary, but she wasn't back yet from the bathroom.

"We are going to have three categories," Mr. Parsons explained. "Best male singer, best female singer, and best couple. We'll start the festivities in a few minutes, so think of the song you want to sing and get ready!"

The band started back up again. Kyle looked around impatiently for Hillary. He wanted to tell her that it was time to go home.

"Kyle. Hey."

Someone sat down on the couch next to him. And for once, it wasn't a girl but Declan McDonough. He was dressed in a black, scratchy cloak that went to his ankles and had green, glowing makeup all over his face. He had hooked a giant scythe around the back of the couch.

"Hey," Kyle said back. "Who are you supposed to be?"

"The grim reaper," Declan said. Kyle stared at him blankly. "You know, the guy who collects your soul when you die?"

Kyle widened his eyes. "There's a guy that *does* that?"

Declan smiled crookedly. "Well, no. Not literally. At least I don't think so." He leaned back. "Have you seen Lori?" Declan asked. "I've been looking for her all night."

Kyle shook his head. "She's not here. She decided to stay home."

Declan looked flabbergasted. "She did? Why?"

Kyle stared at him. He thought about Lori's dejected and lonely look before she'd disappeared back into her bedroom. How she'd started crying in the courtyard the other day, when she admitted to Kyle that she liked Declan but hated herself for it. Lori had asked him not to say anything to Declan, and Kyle didn't want to break his promise. Only, what good had saying nothing done? Kyle hadn't said anything to Amanda. He'd pretended to be someone he wasn't. And look where it was getting him—nowhere.

Kyle took a deep breath. "Lori stayed home because she thought you had a date," he blurted out.

Declan raised one eyebrow. "Huh?"

"She felt uncomfortable," Kyle said. "And . . . hurt." His took in Declan's irritated expression. He hoped he was doing the right thing.

"But I don't have a date," Declan said slowly. "I *told* her I wasn't bringing a date. Why didn't she believe me?"

"It was on someone's blog," Kyle said. "I think that's how she found out."

Declan paused, thinking. He scoffed. "Who believes anything on a blog?" He rubbed his eyes. "She really stayed home because of me, huh?"

"I think so," Kyle said in a small voice.

"I thought she hated me," Declan said softly, staring off into the distance.

Kyle heaved a sigh. "Well, sometimes people do one thing but mean the complete opposite." He fiddled with the white mask in his hands. "Lori's home alone tonight. Her parents went to a party down the street. Maybe you should pay her a visit."

Declan gave Kyle a suspicious look. "She'll just tell me to go away."

Kyle shook his head. "I don't think so."

Declan stood up. "Well . . . okay," he said. He patted Kyle's shoulder and smiled. "Thanks."

"You're welcome," Kyle said.

He watched Declan snake through the crowd of kids, past Kyle's gigantic, spooky mural and out the front door. He smiled to himself and felt a warm, satisfied feeling inside. Hopefully, this would turn Lori's night around.

"Okay, it looks like we're ready," Parsons called from the stage. "Everyone who wants to sing for the title of best couple, come on up!"

Suddenly Hillary stood above him, her hair fluffed and her makeup reapplied. "*There* you are." She grabbed his hand. "Come on. We're competing. We're the cutest people here, I have a great singing voice, and we're definitely going to win."

Kyle shut his eyes. "I think I'll pass," he said. The last thing he wanted to do was get on a stage.

"Come *on*." Hillary pulled him up. "I have the perfect song. It's a duet. You don't have to know the words. The karaoke machine provides them for you."

Suddenly Kyle noticed two people climbing up the risers to the stage. He gasped. It was Amanda and Charlie.

Hillary spied them, too. "See? *That* is exactly why we need to compete."

Kyle stumbled behind Hillary in a daze. When the bright stage lights hit him, he felt woozy. Suddenly he was climbing up the stairs and standing on the wood stage, next to a giant amplifier, a couple dressed up as two people from *Star Trek*, and . . . Amanda.

When Amanda saw Kyle, she did a double take. "Oh my God, Kyle!" she cried, breaking into a huge smile. "I've been looking for you all night!"

"You have?" Kyle asked.

"Absolutely!" She looked Kyle up and down. "You look great!"

"Thanks," Kyle said. He bit his lip and tilted his head. "I'm sorry, though. Who are you guys supposed to be?"

Charlie stepped forward. "Bonnie and Clyde, of course."

"Who?" Kyle asked.

"Only the most famous bank robbing couple?" Charlie looked annoyed.

"You might not have read about them in your encyclopedias," Amanda whispered, winking.

"Come on, Amanda," Charlie said gruffly. "We need to give Parsons our names and figure out what to sing."

But Amanda lagged behind. She peered at Kyle curiously—and then at Hillary, who had her arms wrapped around Kyle's waist. Amanda's eyes slid up and down Hillary's skimpy dress and bare legs. "Wait. Are you two here together?"

"That's right," Hillary said loudly, nuzzling up to Kyle's cheek. "Kyle asked me to go with him the other day."

Amanda looked at Kyle with disbelief. Her expression seemed to say *You asked Hillary?* She took a step backward, colliding with a microphone stand. It seemed as if Kyle had literally knocked her off balance.

Kyle started to open his mouth, but Hillary talked over him. "We have been having So. Much. Fun," she said. "Are you and *Charlie* having fun, Amanda?"

"I . . . guess . . ." Amanda croaked.

"Good!" Hillary crowed. "We're going to sing something really sexy. I'm so psyched."

Kyle watched as Amanda's face simmered with disbelief. Then her expression bled into one of disappointment. And then . . . sadness. Her eyes pulled down and her mouth twisted and pursed.

Finally she looked away. "Well, that's great, guys," she said in a small, tortured voice. "I hope you win cutest couple. It certainly looks like you deserve it."

With that, Amanda turned and walked back to Charlie, her shoulders rigid and her face taut. She whispered something into Charlie's ear. Charlie looked annoyed and whispered something back. Amanda shook her head, glanced quickly at Kyle and Hillary, and then abruptly skittered off the stage. She elbowed through the crowd until Kyle couldn't see her anymore. Charlie sighed audibly and stomped off the stage, going in the completely opposite direction.

Hillary looked at Kyle excitedly. "Oh. My. God. Did you *see* her face! And now she's leaving! Kyle, it's working!"

Kyle ran his hand nervously over the points on top of his Prince Charming crown. It didn't seem like anything was working. Amanda seemed upset . . . at him. "Maybe I should go talk to her," he murmured.

"God, Kyle," Hillary mumbled. "Don't be so impatient. Let her come to *you*. She will. I promise. The wheels in her head are already turning." She rotated her finger in the air to imitate a wheel spinning around.

Kyle looked at Hillary, suddenly irritated. This was nothing but a big game to her. But to Kyle, it was serious. Important. Scary. "I think Operation Make Her

Jealous is officially done," he said. He walked off the stage, too, leaving Hillary standing by herself.

But when Kyle stepped off the last riser, he lost his bearings. He couldn't remember which way Amanda haBd gone and had no ideALa how far she'd gotteLn. Kyle darAted riNght and leTft, past the drinIks table Nand around the haunEted house. He looked right and left for Amanda's black beret . . . but she was gone.

19. Don't Fear the Reaper

The sky had turned from a dusky purple to a deep plum to an inky black. Tom Foss drank the dregs of coffee at the bottom of a mug, placed it on his desk, and stood up.

It was time to go. Time for this to be over.

Suddenly he noticed something in one of the corner monitors. A shadowy shape entered the Trager kitchen and walked over to the fridge. Foss sat back down. It was Lori, the girl. But what was she doing home? Foss had been certain he'd seen three teenagers leave earlier. Now he watched as she peered inside the fridge, grabbed a soda, and slammed the door shut.

Foss tapped his chin, thinking. He had no choice—he *had* to do this tonight. They were running out of time. He watched as Lori drained her can of soda and tossed it into the recycling bin under the sink. Then she strode out of the kitchen, into the hall, and onto the couch in the den. Foss followed her on the monitors the whole way.

Lori switched on the television and started surfing the billions of cable channels. Some night this was. So far, she'd spent nearly two hours sitting in her bedroom, watching the trick-or-treaters walk up and down the sidewalk. They approached her house and looked suspiciously at the darkened door. Some rang the doorbell anyway. Some noticed the basket of candy Lori's parents had set on the porch, reached in, and grabbed more than one piece. For a moment, she wished she were young enough to be trick-or-treating, too. Things were so much simpler then.

She tried not to think about what was happening at the Mash, but couldn't exactly help it. The Mash kept pretty much to the same schedule every year: there was haunted house touring and pictures during the first hour, the karaoke contest the second hour, and hard-core dancing the final hour. Right now, they were probably smack in the middle of the karaoke contest. Lori wondered if Declan and whoever his date was had competed for best couple. Probably. They'd probably won, too—unless Kyle and Hillary had. Hillary adored karaoke, and she'd probably dragged Kyle up there with her.

Suddenly Lori felt like she heard something. She muted the TV. The house was silent. Everything looked the same as it had earlier today. All the knick-knacks on the bookcases were in their exact same places, all the pillows on the easy chair were fluffed and neatly arranged, all the pictures on the wall hung straight. Only, she had the oddest feeling . . . like someone was watching her.

She stood up and walked into the hall. "Hello?" she called. She spun around. "Hello?"

Tom Foss stared at Lori on his monitor. *What was she doing?* he wondered. It looked like she was yelling straight at the camera.

His mind churned. Was it possible Lori knew about the fob? Maybe she knew where Kyle had hidden it. If Kyle didn't respond to threats, perhaps Lori did. And she *was* home alone . . .

Use whatever force necessary, Foss thought. But . . . no.

This wasn't the right time to return to the house. There would be a better time . . . soon.

Lori listened to the sound of her shallow breathing echoing off the walls. She had to be crazy. Just because there was some creepy guy poking around in their bushes the other day didn't mean he was back tonight. She could call her parents . . . and say what? *Hey, Mom and Dad. I'm scared . . . for no good reason. I just need you to come home and tuck me in.* Her night was pathetic enough as it was.

When the doorbell rang, she let out a little yelp. It was too late for the trick-or-treaters to be out . . . so did that mean it could be that strange guy? Would he be so stupid as to come to the door? Or perhaps it was all some sort of setup. Lori looked around frantically, then ran up the stairs and ducked into Josh's bedroom, canvasing the room for some sort of weapon. Amazingly, video gameaholic Josh had a wooden baseball bat next to his bureau. She grabbed it—if whoever it was at the door tried to hurt her, she could whack him over the head with it. At the last minute, she grabbed Josh's bike helmet and put it on her head. Extra protection never hurt.

She slowly crept down the stairs. The person's head rippled behind the front door's frosted glass panels. The doorbell rang again, and Lori let out a little whimper. She put her hand on the doorknob, opened the door a tiny crack, and looked out. The grim reaper was staring at her.

Lori screamed and raised the bat over her head.

"Lori?" a familiar voice called. "Lori, wait. It's me."

Lori frowned. The scream froze in her throat. She stared at the hooded figure. *"Declan?"*

She opened the door a little more. It *was* Declan. He was dressed in a long, shadowy cape and held a grim reaper scythe.

"Get inside," she blurted to Declan, unlatching the door and pulling him into the foyer.

"What are you doing?" Declan whirled into the hall and looked at her curiously. "Why are you wearing a bike helmet?"

Lori stepped back. Suddenly she realized she was acting ridiculous. She quickly undid the helmet's strap and took it off. Then she walked into her dad's office and slumped down on the couch next to his computer. "Forget it. It's a long story."

Then she realized something else. Her head shot up. "Wait a minute. What are you doing here?"

Declan blinked. He followed Lori into the office and sat down behind her dad's desk. "I—I came to see you. You weren't at the Monster Mash."

Lori made a wry face. *What, did your date suck that badly?* she wanted to ask. She was about to say it when Declan held up his hand. "I didn't have a date, Lori."

Lori's mouth fell open. Now Declan was a mind reader, too?

"I wanted to take you to the Mash," Declan explained. "Only . . . you've been acting so weird, I sort of thought you hated me. I was going to ask you when we were playing volleyball in gym, but I felt like it was the wrong moment—there were all those kids around, we were all sweaty, I don't know. And then you got so angry . . ."

"I thought you were blowing me off," Lori admitted. "I was mad."

Declan didn't say anything for a moment. He stared

at the office carpet, which had a tiny coffee stain near one of the desk's wooden legs. "I know the sex thing was . . ."

"Awful," Lori finished for him.

"I was going to say awkward," Declan said. "And maybe it shouldn't have happened. I don't know. But Hillary was wrong about what she said—about me asking you out because—because I thought you'd do it. I asked you out because I wanted to hang out with you. Really."

Lori didn't answer. She just sat on the couch, staring absently at her fingernails.

"After that, when we didn't talk for a while, I started to really miss you," Declan went on. "And not just because we were hooking up, either. I liked hanging out with you. We used to have fun. And suddenly, that was just . . . gone."

"Yeah," Lori said in a small voice.

Declan sighed. "So. I guess I'll ask you what I should've asked you the other day in the gym. Do you want to go to the Monster Mash with me?"

Lori wrinkled her nose. "It's probably almost over."

Declan pulled up the sleeve of his reaper robe and checked his watch. "There's an hour and a half left. I heard the haunted house is really spooky this year. Maybe we could tour it together."

Lori's shoulders rose and fell. "I've had enough scares for one night, thanks." She stood. "But all right. I'll go with you. As friends."

"Of course," Declan said quickly.

Lori nodded. She wasn't quite ready to admit how she truly felt about Declan—not tonight, anyway. But by the way Declan was staring at her, she wondered if he had beyond-friends feelings for her, too. Maybe, just maybe, he did.

She told Declan she'd be ready in a few minutes—she just had to change. She walked upstairs and shut the bedroom door. Her sexy cat outfit swung on its hanger. Then Lori had a thought. She opened her closet. At the back, behind all her shoes, was the box marked OLD COSTUMES. She pulled out the box, opened it, and found what she was looking for right away. She slid the drapey dress over her shoulders and positioned the wig on her head. The fishnets had holes in them, but it didn't really matter. Finally, she lined dark circles around her eyes and grabbed the ratty old broom at the bottom of the box.

She stared at herself in the mirror. Suddenly Declan appeared behind her. Lori jumped—she still wasn't used to him in his reaper cape. "You look *scary*," he said.

"I'm a dead witch," Lori exclaimed, waving around her broom.

"I love it," Declan said. He extended his arm. "Come on, Ms. Witch."

"Gladly, Mr. Reaper," Lori said.

They walked down the stairs. Lori caught a glimpse of herself in the hall mirror. She looked ghoulish and ghastly . . . absolutely not sexy. A few days ago, Lori would have never fathomed wearing this outfit again—it broke every rule in Hillary's How to Make Him Want You book. But she wondered if Hillary's rules applied to her anymore. She curled her fingers around Declan's hand and squeezed. He squeezed back.

"I'm really glad I ran into Kyle and he told me to

come find you," Declan said as they were walking down the front steps to Declan's car.

"Kyle?" Lori stopped, feeling a bristle of anger. Hadn't she told Kyle *not* to say anything?

But then she sighed. Who was she kidding? "Yeah, I'm glad he told you to find me, too."

Foss watched as the two of them exited the foyer and walked down the front path. Okay, *now* everyone in the house was gone. He flipped back to the screen that showed Kyle's bedroom and slowly began to move the camera this way and that, looking at the desk, the tub, the floor. As far as he could tell, the fob wasn't in there.

Which meant, then, that the fob was with Kyle. Foss hoped he could get it back . . . before it was too late.

20. The Masked Man

Amanda was really, truly gone. Kyle had scoured the Mash for her, even poking his head into the girls' bathroom to call her name. She must have left.

Kyle slumped down on a chair near the haunted house. Suddenly a shadow loomed over him. When he looked up, he saw Hillary leaning against a large zombie mannequin. Her shoulders rose and fell. She had a sheepish look on her face. "Hey," she said quietly.

"Hey," Kyle answered glumly.

Hillary sat down next to him. The band's bass was turned up so loud, it made the floor vibrate. Every so often, they'd hear a "booooo" from inside the haunted house, and then someone would scream. Hillary let out a sigh. "From the look on your face, I would say that you don't think Operation Make Her Jealous is going very well."

Kyle shrugged. He couldn't get Amanda's look of disappointment when Kyle had told her he and Hillary were together out of his head. "I guess not," he decided.

"You really freaked out when Amanda took off," Hillary pointed out.

Kyle shrugged. "I hated lying to Amanda's face. I mean, even if it made her jealous, it didn't feel very good. I think I just want to be honest with her."

Hillary fiddled with the rhinestone rings on her fingers. She must have respritzed herself with perfume recently, because Kyle's nose tickled every time she moved. "You're really sweet, Kyle," she said suddenly.

Kyle looked up at her. Hillary's face was soft and almost demure. "Thanks," he said. "Although . . . I don't really *feel* that sweet."

Hillary looked away, biting her lip. "Not that this matters, but since everybody's all into honesty and everything, I'm going to let you in on a little secret. You have a crush on Amanda . . . but I have a crush on you."

Kyle stared at her. "You . . . do?"

Hillary nodded slowly. "A big, mammoth crush, actually. It's pretty embarrassing. I wasn't going to tell you, because I didn't want to, like, ruin things. But . . . I don't know. I thought maybe I'd give it a shot."

Kyle didn't know what to say. Hillary looked embarrassed, completely unconfident, and . . . well, nothing like herself. She kept biting her fingernails and fiddling with her jewelry. Kyle wondered if this was the first honest, vulnerable thing Hillary had ever said to anyone.

"You don't have to do anything about it," Hillary said. "I mean, I like lots of guys. It's just . . . usually I don't tell them. Not directly, anyway. I play Operation Make Him Jealous. Or my various other games. Sometimes they work, sometimes they don't." She smiled, embarrassed. "You really like Amanda, don't you?"

Kyle nodded.

Hillary shrugged. "Are you in *love*?"

Kyle shrugged. "I don't know. I'm not sure what love feels like."

Hillary thought for a moment. "I've never really been in love, so I don't know either. But I think it goes like this: when you like someone, you want to play games. When you love him, you don't."

Kyle sat back. He hadn't given much thought to love. He thought he understood the kind of love parents had for their kids and kids had for their parents—surely *he'd* loved his own parents, whoever they were, in the same way. And he thought he understood what people meant by romantic love—he saw it when he caught Nicole and Stephen cuddled on the couch together. He'd never applied that sort of love to himself, however. There were so many other things he needed to understand first that love had sort of fallen between the cracks.

But by Hillary's definition, maybe Kyle did love Amanda. He chewed on his thumbnail, letting it sink in. It seemed almost right. But it also made him sad. Amanda wasn't his.

He turned to Hillary. She was slowly reapplying her lipstick. "Thanks for telling me . . . what you just told me," he said. "It was really brave of you."

"You're welcome," Hillary said. She thought for a moment. "It was interesting. A little freaky but kind of cool."

"So are you going to be honest with people now?" Kyle asked hopefully.

Hillary rolled her eyes. "Doubt it." She tapped Kyle flirtatiously on the nose. "You have your way of dealing with stuff and I have mine."

"Well, I guess I tried," Kyle said. They grinned at each other. And suddenly Kyle realized—through all this, he'd actually gotten to know Hillary beyond her tough, flirtatious, man-eating exterior. He'd discovered she hid things—her insecurities, her weaknesses, and her crushes—just like everyone else.

The band launched into "The Monster Mash," and everyone in the audience jumped around and screamed. Kyle, however, felt deflated. He wanted to be alone with his thoughts. He stood up and mumbled to Hillary that he needed to get a little air. He noticed a doorway marked TO ROOF and went through it.

The narrow stairs were dark and a little murky, one of the few places Kyle and Amanda hadn't decorated. He climbed up until he emerged on the rec center's roof. All Seattle twinkled around him. He could see the boats on the harbor and all the tall buildings of downtown. The air was cool and crisp, not stifling and humid like it was inside.

But he wasn't alone. Clumps of kids sat all around the roof, laughing and talking. A couple was kissing, and then another couple. Kyle caught sight of Josh cuddling with a girl in a silvery bodysuit. He realized it was Ashleigh, the girl from Jeff Preston's party. The girl whispered something in Josh's ear, and Josh laughed. Kyle smiled to himself. Josh seemed really comfortable with her.

Kyle considered going over to say hi, but decided against it. He wanted to be invisible right now. Alone with his thoughts. He found his mask in his pocket. It felt cool and right over his face. No one even looked at him. It was like he'd put on a cloak that hid him completely. He wished he would've thought to put this on a lot earlier.

Suddenly a tall boy dressed as a *Star Wars* Jedi stood up. "That's *not* what I said!" he screamed to his friend.

"Yes, you *did*!" A boy dressed as a gorilla stood, too. He shoved the Jedi. "I can take you."

Kyle bristled. Suddenly, the two boys were really going at it. They both looked hostile and drunk. A crowd quickly gathered. A couple of guys tried to break them up, but the fighters just pushed them away. They continued to shove each other, struggling in their costumes, knocking into other people. Kyle took a few steps back toward the roof's edge, trying to keep his distance. Josh and Ashleigh also stood up, looking concerned. The fighters were shoving each other so vigorously, they were flailing dangerously close to the roof's ledge. Josh took Ashleigh's arm and guided her around them. Josh noticed Kyle, and snaked through the crowd so they could all stand together. For a moment, they all stood transfixed on the raised ledge that bordered the roof deck, watching the fighters shove each other. Suddenly one of the fighters careened out of the circle. He knocked straight into Ashleigh and Kyle . . . and suddenly, they were falling.

Ashleigh screamed. Kyle's body reacted before his mind did. He grabbed Ashleigh's waist and pulled her close to him. The distance from the roof to the ground was greater than the jump from the tree in his backyard, and Kyle landed awkwardly on his back, with Ashleigh on top of him. All his bones shook and he let out a loud groan.

Ashleigh crawled off Kyle, and they both stood up. They were miraculously okay. Ashleigh looked amazedly around the parking lot as if they'd just landed on the moon.

"W-what happened?" she stammered.

Kyle breathed heavily. He wasn't sure what to say.

Everyone on the roof had gathered at the ledge. Kyle could hear people yelling, shocked. "She fell right on top of him!" one girl cried, disbelief clear in her voice.

"But they're both okay!" someone else said.

"But that's impossible," another guy argued. "It's like four stories or something."

Ashleigh looked back at Kyle. Her mouth fell open. "How did you . . . ?"

"Does anybody know that guy?" someone called from above.

"Who was the girl that fell?"

"Ashleigh?" called a familiar voice. Kyle watched as Josh's wide Zorro hat appeared at the front of the crowd. Josh peered over the edge. "Are you all right?"

Ashleigh waved back at Josh. "Yeah, I'm cool," she said shakily.

"Who *is* that dude?" someone said.

"Take your mask off, man!" a guy instructed.

"What school do you go to?" a girl screamed.

"Hey, Prince!" someone called. "What's your name?"

Ashleigh looked at Kyle. "Yeah, what *is* your name?" she asked. "You seem familiar."

Kyle took a step back. He knew this was unusual. And that he should keep it quiet. He glanced up at the crowd on the roof once more. There was only one person up there who knew who had saved Ashleigh—Josh. Kyle met Josh's eyes. Josh looked proud of him. He mouthed *thanks*.

Kyle nodded, and then looked back at Ashleigh. He ran his fingers over his face mask, making sure it was still there. It was, thankfully. "I have to go," he blurted out, and then ran as fast as he could across the parking lot, into the darkness.

21. A Moment
of Brilliance

Josh held Ashleigh's arm as they carefully walked back inside. Ashleigh was still stunned from her fall and kind of raving. "I mean, suddenly I was pushed over the edge!" she cried. "And then, I felt this arm reaching for me. He grabbed me in *midair* and wrapped his arms around me! I didn't even know someone could do that!"

"Oh, Kyle can do that, all right," Josh murmured.

Ashleigh looked up sharply. "What?"

"Nothing," Josh said quickly.

"Anyway, I wish I knew who saved me," she murmured, smoothing down her hair and checking the back of her stockings once again for any runs. "I didn't even get a good look at him, I was so out of it. Why do you think he ran away like that?"

Josh didn't answer. He didn't want to give anything away. He knew as well as Kyle did that Kyle should probably keep his talents a secret—it might draw attention to him he didn't want. Then again, he was happy Kyle had been the one to fall with Ashleigh. He was happy he saved her. If Kyle hadn't, Ashleigh might be . . .

He shut his eyes, trying not to think about it.

Then Josh noticed someone in the distance. "Check it out," he murmured to himself. "Lori's here. And she looks like a freak."

Up ahead, Lori and Declan wove through the crowd. Lori wore a drapey, spidery dress, a large pointed hat, and had black circles painted under her eyes. Hillary was with them, too. Josh and Ashleigh joined them.

"Nice costume," Ashleigh said to Lori, admiring her outfit.

Lori rolled her eyes. "I know, I know, I don't look hot. Guys are vomiting when they see me. Hillary's already given me the lecture."

"I'm in mourning," Hillary said dramatically. "Lori has gone over to the dark side."

"No, I'm serious," Ashleigh said. "I really like it. It's really scary. And Halloween's supposed to be scary, right?"

"I think so." Lori smiled at Ashleigh. "Thanks."

"Hey."

Kyle had materialized in front of them. His mask was off, and he'd removed his medals, purple vest, and crown. "Hey," Josh said. "Ashleigh. This is my foster brother, Kyle."

Kyle reached out his hand, his heart pounding. He hoped Ashleigh wouldn't recognize him. "Nice to meet you."

"Likewise," Ashleigh said softly. She looked at him oddly for a moment and then looked away. Kyle met Josh's eyes, and they exchanged a secret, appreciative smile.

Hillary touched Kyle's arm. "Where have you been? I've been looking for you."

Kyle groaned. "I told you. Operation Make Her Jealous is over."

Hillary shook her head. "I've been looking for you for *her*." She stepped away and gestured across the room. Amanda was standing in front of their mural. She gave Kyle a little wave, and Kyle's stomach turned over.

"I found her earlier," Hillary whispered. "I told her we came here just as friends. You should go talk to her."

Kyle looked at Hillary. "I should?"

Hillary shrugged. "You said it yourself. Operation Make Her Jealous is officially done."

Kyle took a deep breath. His eyes met Amanda's, and he waved her over. She floated across the room. "Hi, Kyle," she said.

Kyle suddenly felt nervous. He wasn't sure what he wanted to say to Amanda. Did she suspect what he'd been doing all night? Why had she run off the stage? Was she angry? Instead, he blurted out, "Where's Charlie?"

Amanda shrugged, looking uncomfortable. "I don't know. Doing something with his friends."

"Oh."

The band melted into a slow song. Everyone started to pair up. Kyle felt Amanda looking at him. He put his hands in his pockets, then took them out again. Out of the corner of his eye, he saw Hillary waving her arms around. "Ask her," she was mouthing. "Ask her to dance."

"Do you want to dance?" Kyle asked Amanda, his voice cracking on *dance*.

"Um, okay," Amanda said in a small, shy voice.

Kyle wrapped his arms around Amanda's waist. She put her arms around his neck. She smelled just like she did the other day, like honeysuckle and soap. They slowly swayed back and forth, not saying anything. Kyle tried to get his breathing to slow down, but it was difficult. He'd yearned for this moment all night. Now it was here. And now he felt freaked out.

Amanda stood back and looked into Kyle's eyes. "So why have you been ignoring me all night?"

Kyle blinked. "I haven't been ignoring you."

"Yes, you have." Amanda looked hurt. "I kept seeing you across the room. I'd wave, but you wouldn't look over. You were always with Hillary. And then on the stage . . . you guys were acting so weird. She was all over you . . . and . . . I don't know." Amanda pursed her lips. "This might sound weird, but I felt like I didn't even know you. Like you were a total stranger."

Kyle's brain buzzed. "We're not really together," he said.

"Hillary said that, too. You're really . . . not?"

Kyle swallowed hard. "We came here together, but we're not a couple."

"Oh." Amanda's voice lifted. She sounded almost . . . pleased. "So . . . Hillary's *not* your type, then."

Kyle's heart pounded. The moment seemed to stretch on forever. Kyle was aching to tell Amanda how he felt. He knew he should keep his feelings for her a secret—but he was so tired of keeping secrets.

No, he had to be honest with her. He needed to be honest about a lot of things. Like that Foss knew his name and that Kyle had found Foss's key fob. The Monster Mash had taught him one very important lesson—some things he couldn't hide, no matter what.

Amanda's lips parted. Kyle's heart hammered away. Slowly he leaned down and put his mouth to Amanda's ear. "No, Hillary's not my type," he said softly, loud enough so that only she could hear. "No one's my type. Except . . . you."

Amanda let go of his neck and stepped back. She

blinked furiously, as if she were waking up from a dream. At first, she looked shocked, but then she looked . . . scared. And pleased. And overwhelmed. Her face showed a million things at once. She opened her mouth to speak.

Suddenly Charlie was behind them. He whipped Amanda's beret off her head. "There you are."

"Oh!" Amanda cried, in a loud, terrified voice.

Charlie took Amanda's arm. He glanced at Kyle. "Do you mind? I heard this was the last slow song of the night."

Kyle stepped back. All the air seemed to leave his body. "Sure," he said hoarsely.

Charlie whisked Amanda away, putting his arm around her and whispering in her ear. When they were a few paces away, Amanda turned around and gave Kyle a confused, beseeching, longing look. Kyle stared back. And then she disappeared into the crowd.

Hillary touched Kyle's shoulder. "You told her you liked her, didn't you?" She stared into the throng of dancers.

Kyle nodded faintly.

"And she just . . . left with him?"

Kyle nodded again.

Hillary looked stricken. "Oh, Kyle. Are you okay?"

Kyle thought about it. "I think I am," he said slowly. In some ways, he felt awful—Amanda was with Charlie. And he couldn't believe he'd actually done it. But he was also amazed he'd waited so long. He felt like he'd lifted off the big cinder block that had been sitting on his chest ever since he'd met Amanda. Now she knew. Things would happen, or they wouldn't, but at least Kyle was free.

"Last song of the night!" the singer in the band

crowed into the microphone. They started playing a dance song everyone recognized. Hillary and Lori started to cheer, and the lights snapped off and the black lights flickered on.

Kyle looked around the room. The black lights cast a purplish pall over the dance floor. The only things that stood out were people's teeth, eyes, and fingernails. It was eerie, seeing nothing but a few bits of skin and teeth glowing in a sea of darkness. Hillary grabbed Kyle's hand and pulled him into their dancing circle. Kyle wiggled and swayed, trying to imitate the others, and then shut his eyes and just went with his own rhythm, not caring what he looked like. Feeling as free as possible.

Suddenly his neck started to tingle. A sharp image flashed into his mind. *Foss*. Kyle's eyes snapped open. He looked around, alert. The dance floor was nothing but greenish teeth and glowing hands. Was Foss here? Was Foss watching? He checked the stage, the ceiling, all the exits. He didn't see Foss anywhere.

Still. Kyle felt like his senses were trying to tell him something. Slowly he reached into his pocket and felt for the plastic fob. It was still there. He pulled it out. It felt heavy and dark in his glowing hand. When he turned it over, his mouth fell open.

There were words printed on the back, written in some kind of ink that glowed under the black light. Kyle squinted at the letters. *Mada Corp*.

His heart pounded. Tiny flashes of electricity sparkled in his brain. That name sounded familiar. Why? Was it something from his past? Kyle squeezed his eyes shut, trying to remember. "Mada Corp, Mada Corp," he whispered to himself.

Suddenly Kyle saw himself surrounded by gooey,

pink water. A large sheet of glass separated him from two other people. They peered in at him, as if Kyle was in a fish tank. One of the onlookers was a man who looked eerily like Kyle, and the other was a stern-looking, beefy, frowning man. "Good-bye," the man who looked like Kyle was saying. "That's enough," the stern man said, roughly grabbing his arm. There was a badge on the second man's sleeve. It said MADA CORP.

A third man wearing a security guard's uniform stood in the doorway. He watched the two men carefully as they left the room. Then the guard turned to Kyle and stared at him through the glass. It was *Foss*.

Kyle's eyes snapped open. All around him, kids danced normally, as if nothing out of the ordinary had happened. But Kyle felt dizzy. The vision seemed so *real*. He felt like he had just been there.

As the song wound down, the black lights snapped off. Kyle looked at the key fob. The Mada Corp words were gone again. Hidden. He backed out of the circle. He was glad this was the last song of the night—he couldn't get home soon enough.

He had to find the answer.

22. What Dreams May Come

A little after midnight, Kyle heard the last light in the kitchen snap off. Slowly, the house settled into silence. When he was certain everyone was asleep, he got up, found the fob in his pocket, and tiptoed over to his laptop.

The computer flickered to life. Kyle put the fob on the desk next to him. He gritted his teeth and waved his hands over the keyboard, thinking. Slowly, he typed *Mada Corp* into the search engine and hit Enter.

There was a site—www.madacorp.com. Kyle held his breath when he clicked the link. This was it—the site that might unveil some big, dangerous secret from his past. It might tell him why Foss needed the fob back so desperately. It might even tell him who he used to be.

The site slowly loaded. MADA CORPORATION appeared on a cool, calming blue banner at the top of the page. Below it, MAKING LIFE BETTER FOR ALL MANKIND swam into view. There was a picture of three ambitious-looking adults. *"Welcome to Mada Corporation . . ."* the text read. *"We are dedicated to the belief that anything is possible. Combining the best of science, technology, the arts and humanities, we have already proven this to be true. And we've only just begun . . ."*

Kyle frowned. This looked like a normal company website. There was an Investor Relations tab with a graph of Mada Corp.'s financial progress from 1971 to the present. A listing of projects around different areas of the globe. Kyle tried a few other tabs—Current Projects—but the information was confidential. There was an employee log-in screen at the corner of every page, and Kyle tried various user names—*FossT, TomFoss, Kyle*—and entered the random six digits on the key fob. Each time, however, the same window came up. *Access Denied. You are not authorized to view this page. A report has been sent to Mada Corporation regarding your request.*

Kyle's heart sank. This wasn't what he thought it would be. It just looked like a bland and corporate business page—nothing here was scary or sinister. Maybe the key fob simply unlocked someone's corporate e-mail account, or perhaps some investment data. And this page didn't look familiar in the slightest. Nothing here seemed to trigger any memories about the past.

Suddenly Kyle felt the prickly feeling at the back of his neck again. He turned around, his heart pounding. No one was in his bedroom doorway. Or at the window. He glanced at the closet. It was shut. He stared at the upper corner of the room, behind the door. The feeling became even stronger. But the only thing that was there was the disk-shaped smoke alarm, its green light steadily blinking. *I'm losing my mind,* he thought.

Sighing, he shut off the computer, put the fob on top of a stack of books, climbed into his tub, and pulled the comforter over him. He felt heavy and numb—like he'd come so close to something, only to have it all slip away. The fob probably wasn't even Foss's. Maybe someone else had dropped it, like a gardener, or someone who had cut through the Tragers' yard. Kyle started to question whether it really was Tom Foss in the yard the other night, or if Kyle's brain simply wanted it to be. Maybe he didn't even know Foss from his past. Although the eerie Mada Corp. memory that had flashed in front of Kyle's brain at the Monster Mash *seemed* like it had happened, he had no idea what was really real anymore.

"Kyle," a voice whispered.

Kyle's eyes sprang open. To his astonishment, Amanda was hovering over him in the tub. Her hair fell all around her face, and the corners of her lips curled into a mesmerizing smile. "Hey," Amanda said.

"W-what are you doing here?" Kyle stammered.

"I came to see you," Amanda said. "I can't stop thinking about what you said at the Mash." She reached forward and, ever so softly, touched Kyle's face. It felt like all the nerve endings on Kyle's cheeks had been dead until this very moment. He shuddered with pleasure.

"I'm so glad you left the window open for me," Amanda said. She started to slide off her sneakers. "Can I get in the tub with you?"

Kyle sat up. "The window was open?" It wasn't when he went to sleep—Kyle always made a point to close and lock it.

"Yes, it was wide open," Amanda said, sounding worried. "What's wrong?"

Kyle looked around. Suddenly, he noticed a shadow in the corner. His heart stopped. The shadow stepped into the light. *Foss.*

"Are you looking for me?" Foss whispered.

"What are you doing here?" Kyle whispered hoarsely.

"I've come for what's mine," Foss answered. He held up the Mada Corp. fob. "That's all."

"Kyle?" Amanda grabbed his arm. "Who's that?"

"Don't tell her, Kyle," Foss warned. "And don't tell the people you're living with. It's better if you don't. It'll just create more complications."

"What do you mean?" Kyle sputtered.

"Sorry." Foss shrugged. He eyed Amanda. "Just to make sure you don't say anything, I'm taking her with me." He grabbed Amanda's arm and pulled her toward him.

"Kyle?" Amanda's eyes were wide and scared. "What's going on?"

"No!" Kyle cried. He leaped forward, but he felt like he was swimming through marshmallow. His limbs couldn't move. His hands flailed uncontrollably. He watched helplessly as Foss pushed the key fob into his pocket and slithered out the window, dragging Amanda behind him. The last thing Kyle saw was Foss staring at him through the windowpane, his eyes wide and a finger to his lips. *Shhh*.

Kyle sat up in his tub. He looked around. His room was dark and quiet. The night light glowed in the corner. The heater made its gentle, whooshing noises. There was no one there.

Had it been a . . . dream?

He shakily ran his hands over his face. His forehead was sweaty. The window was closed. Kyle crumpled against the windowsill and breathed a sigh of relief. It *had* been a dream. Amanda hadn't been here. Neither had Foss. And Foss hadn't dragged her away.

But when Kyle moved over to his desk, something was out of place. The fob. He'd set it on top of two geometry books, hadn't he? He looked behind the books, but it wasn't there, either. Frowning, he got down on his hands and knees, thinking it might have fallen to the floor. Nope. Kyle canvased the whole of his desk, but it was gone.

Gone.

Kyle felt his heart pounding. He looked to the window again. Foss couldn't have gotten in. There was no way.

Or . . . was there?

Tom FoEss swunMg into his dented IpickLup truck and gazYHed at his reflOection in hisL Lrearview mirrorA. He let outN a huge sigh. It haDdn't been eEasy to shimmRy in through Kyle's window—especially while Kyle was asleep. He'd barely gotten out of there in time—as he'd fallen into the bushes, he'd seen Kyle shoot up in his tub, awake and alert.

His cell phone bleated. He grabbed it. "Yeah?"

"Did you get it?" the voice on the other end asked.

"Yes," Foss answered. He stared at the key fob in his palm.

The caller sighed. He sounded exhausted. "Thank God."

"I know," Foss said.

He reached over to his passenger seat and flipped up the monitor of the minireceiver. After hitting a few buttons, the screen fluttered to life. The image zigzagged, then settled, showing Kyle's bedroom. There was Kyle's desk, his chair, his tub bed. Kyle was pacing around the room, confused. As well he should be.

Now Foss rewound the video feed so it showed the events that had occurred just an hour ago. He watched as Kyle sat down at the computer, logged onto the Internet, brought up the Mada Corp. site, and clicked on various tabs. Kyle had been so close . . . and he hadn't even known it. Foss watched as Kyle tinkered around with various passwords, not hitting the right one. And then, Kyle abruptly stopped, turned around, and stared right into the corner where Foss had implanted the hidden camera in the smoke alarm weeks ago. Could Kyle sense the camera's presence? It seemed impossible, but then again . . . this *was* Kyle.

But then, Kyle had shrugged, turned around, and climbed into his tub. Not long after that, Foss had made his move.

"That was close," Foss said to the voice on the phone, "*way* too close."

"We have to end this," the voice told him, "before it's too late."

Foss started up the truck and rolled slowly away from the curb. "I know," he repeated, and hung up. Foss had shown his face to Kyle and threatened him. Now that Foss had stolen back the fob, Kyle could go to the Tragers and report him to the police. Or would Kyle be smart enough to keep quiet? He knew this all had to end. They would have to tell Kyle the truth.

He drove for ten minutes, listening to the sounds of the tires rolling along the road and his shaky, nervous breathing. Finally he came to a deserted parking lot behind an office building. No one would notice him here. He put the truck in park and twisted around to reach under the backseat. The laptop felt cool to the touch. Breathing hard, he pulled it out, set it in his lap, and opened it. As the computer whirred to life, he gazed at the key fob between his fingers. Foss remembered how much of a struggle it had been to steal it out of Mada Corp.'s carefully guarded data room only a few days ago. He remembered darting down the dark halls, diving into Adam's car, and driving away with one eye in the rearview mirror, certain someone would follow them.

But no one had followed. They had gotten the fob—and Kyle and the secrets—out safely.

He logged onto www.madacorp.com. Entered his password in the corner. Typed in the digits in the key fob's window. The computer's little hourglass spun around. And finally the file folder icon appeared on the screen. Foss clicked the right button on his mouse. *Do you want to download files?* a window asked. Foss clicked *Yes*. He watched as the images loaded onto his computer. When it was finished, he hit another button on his computer. *Do you really want to delete files from this account?* the window asked. Foss hit *Yes* for this, too. And in a blink, the files were gone from his Mada Corp. account . . . forever. Foss let out a long, relieved sigh. *Success*. They should have done this as soon as they'd gotten the fob. They had been waiting until the next day . . . but the next day was when Foss had spied on Kyle in his yard and dropped the fob in the bushes. He wouldn't make a mistake like that again.

There were so many things in the file—so many secrets that Kyle couldn't know. Secrets that only Foss could be trusted to keep. Documents, reports, corre-spondence . . . and pictures. Foss clicked on an image marked *in utero*. The picture was of a familiar dark-haired sixteen-year-old boy. He was naked, suspended in a tank of pink, gelatinous goo. Just lying there, com-pletely unresponsive. Unborn. Without a past. The word ZZYZX danced across the door behind the tank. And, in the tank's shimmering reflection, Foss could just barely make out his own face.

Foss slowly closed the lid of the laptop and put the

key fob in his briefcase. He knew it was dangerous for him to do this—Mada Corp. carefully monitored its sites, and soon enough, it would realize someone on the outside had stolen Kyle's secret files. If Mada Corp. sent people after Foss, so be it. He could handle them. If they came after Kyle, on the other hand . . .

Foss leaned back in the truck's bucket seat, shuddering at the thought. If Kyle had been able to access his secret information and Mada Corp. found out—if they found Kyle was alive, *period*—they would destroy him. And that would be the end . . . of everything. All the hard work, all the efforts to cover up Kyle's disappearance, all the stress . . . it would all go down the drain. And so it was Foss's job to make sure that never, *ever* happened.

Even if it meant giving his own life.